Ghosts in the Rear View

A novelization by David Noble

Lulu Press

David Noble

Ghosts in the Rear View

Printed in the United States of America

First Edition

ISBN 979-8-9910855-8-8

Manufactured by Lulu Press, Inc.

700 Park Offices Drive Suite 250 Research Triangle, NC 27709

www.lulu.com

For information about permission to reproduce selections from this book, contact Noble Park Films at info@nobleparkfilms.com

Special Thanks

This is my fifth book and am proud of the results. The idea about this book came in 2010 while living in Louisiana, as part of what seemed to be a never-ending fascination with horror and paranormal themes.

It was during that time that I had the chance to work with creative people like Fred Taulbee, Courtney Shay Young, Elgin Foster, LaTasha Williams, Crystal Tomlin, and others on my first attempt at a feature film called 'Zydeco.' That project is not to be confused with this novel.

'Zydeco' was a much easier project to produce logistically, and so this story that you are about to read was placed on the shelf for a later time. While that time never came for filming, I did find the time to transform the treatment into this book.

I hope you enjoy this story, and I hope you go on your favorite free video streaming service and watch Zydeco right afterwards.

David Noble

Chapter 1
Living in a Small Town

The fluorescent lights of Pete's Diner buzzed incessantly, a grating soundtrack to Josh Hawkins' monotonous existence. At twenty-five, armed with a degree in Native American History from Washburn University, Josh found himself trapped in a cycle of wiping down greasy tables and refilling lukewarm coffee cups.

"Order up, Josh!" Marge's gravelly voice cut through his thoughts. He plastered on a smile, grabbed the plates of steaming eggs and bacon, and made his way to table six.

As he placed the plates down, his eyes caught the headline of a discarded newspaper: "Tech Start-up Brings New Jobs to Topeka." Josh's smile faltered.

Another reminder of opportunities passing him by, of a world moving forward while he remained stuck.

The bell above the diner's door chimed, and Josh's gaze shifted to the newcomer. For a moment, he thought he saw a shadow, more substantial than a mere absence of light, slip in behind the customer. He blinked, and it was gone.

Hours later, Josh fumbled with his keys outside his cramped studio apartment. The lock finally gave way with a reluctant click. He stepped inside, flicking on the lights to reveal a space that seemed to shrink with each passing day. Shelves lined the walls, crammed with books on Native American tribes, rituals, and artifacts. His prized possession, a Sioux dreamcatcher, hung above his bed. Its intricate web of sinew and beads seemed to shimmer in the dim light, as if alive with some inner energy.

Josh collapsed onto his secondhand couch, the weight of student loans and unfulfilled dreams pressing down on him like a physical force. He reached for his laptop, opening it to reveal a familiar sight: job listings in his field, all requiring years of experience he didn't have or located in cities he couldn't afford to move to.

With a sigh, he closed the laptop and leaned back, his eyes drawn to the dreamcatcher. It had been a gift from Dr. Rainwater, his favorite professor, upon graduation. "Remember, Josh," she had said, her eyes twinkling, "our history is alive. It speaks to those who listen."

As if on cue, a whisper seemed to emanate from the dreamcatcher. Josh sat up straight, his heart suddenly racing. He approached the artifact cautiously, studying its familiar contours. That's when he noticed it. A bead, one he could have sworn was blue this morning, now gleamed a deep, arterial red.

Josh reached out, his fingertips barely grazing the surface of the bead. A jolt of electricity shot through him, and for a split second, he wasn't in his apartment anymore. He was standing in a vast, open plain, the air thick with smoke and the metallic scent of blood. Distant screams echoed across the landscape. He jerked his hand back, gasping. The vision vanished, leaving him alone in his apartment once more. But as he stared at the dreamcatcher, a creeping sense of dread settled over him.

Josh shook his head, trying to dispel the lingering unease from his encounter with the dreamcatcher. He glanced at his phone, noticing a text from Mike: "O'Malley's at 9. Don't flake, history boy!"

A mix of emotions washed over him — anticipation, guilt, a touch of resentment. He hadn't seen Mike in weeks, their once-inseparable friendship now stretched thin by the demands of adulthood and the diverging paths of their lives. Josh headed to the bathroom, splashing cold water on his face and studying his reflection. Dark circles underscored his eyes, a testament to late nights spent job hunting and early mornings at the diner. He looked older than his 25 years, worn down by the weight of unfulfilled potential. As he changed into a clean shirt, Josh's mind wandered to his old friend. Mike Harris had been the golden boy of Topeka West High — captain of the football team, prom king, with a full athletic scholarship to K-State in his pocket. But life had a way of derailing even the best-laid plans.

Last Josh had heard, Mike was working at the local plant. The recession had hit Topeka hard, forcing many to abandon their dreams for whatever work they could find. Josh felt a pang of guilt; at least he had managed to finish his degree, even if it seemed useless now. He buttoned up his shirt, rehearsing potential conversations in his head. Would they talk about old times? Or would the gulf between their current lives be too vast to bridge? The thought of facing Mike's inevitable questions about his job search filled Josh with dread.

Returning to the main room, Josh's eyes were drawn once again to the dreamcatcher. The red bead seemed to pulse in the dim light, like a tiny, malevolent heart. He blinked hard, and it was still once more. "Get it together, Hawkins," he muttered, running a hand through his hair.

Josh checked the time — still an hour before he needed to leave for O'Malley's. He sank back onto the couch, his gaze drifting to the stack of Native American history books on his coffee table. On top lay a worn copy of "Lakota Myths and Legends."

Almost without thinking, he picked up the book, flipping to a dog-eared page about dream spirits. As he read, the words seemed to swim before his eyes, rearranging themselves into unfamiliar patterns. A chill ran down his spine as he realized he could no longer understand the text he'd once known by heart. Josh slammed the book shut, his heart racing. The room suddenly felt too small, the air too thick. The walls seemed to press in on him, covered in shadows that writhed and twisted at the corners of his vision.

Josh stood abruptly, grabbing his keys and wallet. Maybe a walk would clear his head before meeting Mike. As he reached for the doorknob, a whisper seemed to emanate from behind him, so faint he might have imagined it: "The past is never dead. It's not even past."

Josh whirled around, but his apartment was empty and still. Only the dreamcatcher moved, swaying gently as if stirred by an unfelt breeze. With a shaky breath, Josh wrenched open the door and stepped out into the hallway. As he pulled the door shut behind him, he couldn't shake the feeling that something had fundamentally changed — that by the time he returned, his world would never be the same.

The night air hit him like a slap to the face as he exited his building, grounding him in reality. Topeka's streets stretched before him, familiar and mundane. But as Josh set off toward O'Malley's, the shadows seemed to lengthen, reaching for him with every step. Somewhere in the distance, a clock tower began to toll the hour, its deep resonance echoing through the empty streets. Josh quickened his pace, unaware that with each chime, the boundary between his world and something far more ancient — and far more terrifying — was growing thinner.

Josh's hand hesitated on the door of his beat-up Corolla. The idea of walking suddenly seemed foolish — Topeka's streets stretched long and dark, and O'Malley's was clear across town. With a sigh, he slid into the driver's seat, the familiar creak of worn leather oddly comforting. As he navigated the quiet streets, memories washed over him like old photographs, sepia-toned and fraying at the edges. He passed Gage Park, where he and Mike had spent countless summer days in their teens, tossing a football and dreaming of futures that seemed boundless.

"You'll be the next Ken Burns, Josh," Mike had once said, sprawled on the sun-warmed grass. "Making documentaries about all that history stuff you love. And I'll be the next Patrick Mahomes."

Josh's grip tightened on the steering wheel. How quickly dreams could curdle into regrets. He turned onto 6th Avenue, the streetlights casting intermittent pools of yellowed light. To his right, Topeka High School loomed, a gothic fortress of brick and memories. It was here, on the worn steps of the main entrance, that he'd first kissed Daria Chen.

Daria. The name alone sent a bittersweet pang through his chest. She'd been his first love — brilliant, fierce, with ambitions that dwarfed the Kansas sky. They'd been inseparable throughout high school, united by a shared desire to escape the gravitational pull of their hometown.

Josh could still picture her on graduation day, radiant in her blue gown, valedictorian medal glinting in the May sunshine. "We're going to change the world," she'd whispered, squeezing his hand.

But life had other plans. Daria had won a full ride to Columbia, her ticket out of Kansas. Josh, hobbled by family obligations and financial constraints, had stayed behind. They'd tried long distance for a while, but the miles and diverging lives proved too much. Last he'd heard, she was in grad school, on track to become the environmental lawyer she'd always dreamed of being. The light turned red, and Josh came to a stop, watching a lone figure hurry across the crosswalk, collar turned up against the night chill. For a moment, he thought he saw Daria's face, but it was just a trick of shadow and streetlight.

As he drove on, the radio crackled to life of its own accord. Through the static, he could have sworn he heard Daria's laugh, followed by Mike's booming voice. Josh jabbed at the power button, plunging the car into silence. But the quiet felt charged now, expectant. He turned onto the street where O'Malley's sat, its neon sign a beacon in the gathering darkness. As he pulled into the parking lot, Josh caught a glimpse of something in his rearview mirror — a shadow, more substantial than the absence of light, flitting between the parked cars.

He blinked, and it was gone. Just another trick of the mind, he told himself, like the whispers in his apartment and Daria's ghost in the crosswalk. Josh killed the engine, but didn't immediately get out. He sat for a moment, forehead resting on the steering wheel, trying to steel himself for the evening ahead. How could he face Mike, embodiment of all their shared and broken dreams? But as he raised his head, resolve hardening, he noticed something odd. The dreamcatcher he kept hanging from his rearview mirror was spinning slowly, though there was no breeze in the closed car. And at its center, a bead gleamed red in the reflected neon light, pulsing like a distant, winking eye.

With a shudder, Josh wrenched the door open and all but fell out of the car. The cool night air hit him like a slap, grounding him in reality. O'Malley's door stood before him, muffled laughter and the clink of glasses spilling out onto the sidewalk. Josh took a deep breath and stepped forward. As he reached for the door handle, he failed to notice the shadow that detached itself from the darkness behind his car, following him with silent, patient hunger.

Chapter 2
The Former Flame

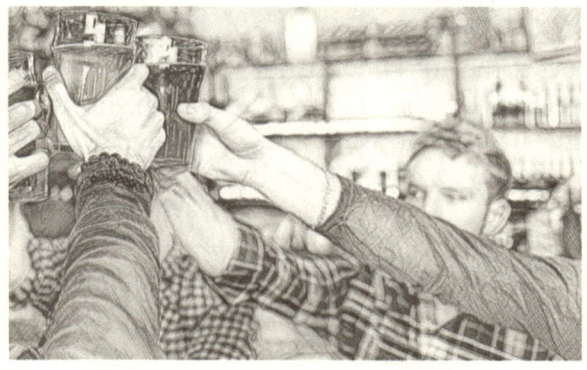

The heavy wooden door of O'Malley's creaked open, unleashing a wave of warmth, noise, and the pungent scent of stale beer. Josh blinked, his eyes adjusting to the dim interior. The bar was crowded for a weeknight, a sea of familiar faces seeking solace in alcohol and companionship. Josh scanned the room, searching for Mike's broad-shouldered silhouette.

A hand shot up from a booth near the back, followed by a booming voice that cut through the din. "Josh! Over here, man!"

Mike's grin was visible even from across the room, a beacon of familiar comfort. Josh weaved through the crowd, nodding at a few acquaintances as he passed. He was almost at the booth when Mike's expression shifted, eyes widening slightly as he glanced over Josh's shoulder.

"Dude," Mike said, his voice lowered as Josh slid into the seat opposite him. "Don't look now, but guess who's in the corner?"

Of course, the instruction not to look only made the urge to turn around nearly irresistible. Josh resisted, focusing instead on Mike's face, noting the new lines around his eyes, the slight shadow of stubble on his jaw.

"Who?" Josh asked, though a part of him already knew the answer, a cold weight settling in his stomach.

Mike leaned in, his voice barely audible over the jukebox. "Daria. She's with some friends in the back corner."

The name hit Josh like a physical blow, confirming his suspicion. He fought the urge to whip around and stare, instead taking a slow, deliberate breath.

"Daria?" he repeated, hating the way his voice cracked slightly on the name. "What's she doing back in Topeka?"

Mike shrugged, signaling to a passing waitress for two beers. "No idea, man. First time I've seen her since... well, you know."

Josh did know. The last time Daria had been in Topeka was the Christmas break after their freshman year of college. The night they'd officially ended things, tearful promises to stay friends evaporating like mist in the harsh light of dawn.

"You gonna say hi?" Mike asked, studying Josh's face with concern.

Before Josh could answer, the waitress arrived with their beers. He took a long pull from the bottle, the cold liquid doing little to dislodge the lump in his throat.

"I don't know," he finally said, absently peeling at the label on his bottle. "It's been years, Mike. She's probably moved on, living that big city life she always wanted."

Mike's eyebrows shot up, a knowing smirk playing at his lips. "Oh yeah? Then why's she keeps looking over here?"

This time, Josh couldn't help himself. He turned, his eyes immediately finding Daria in the crowded bar. She sat with three other women, all of them dressed in business casual, an incongruous sight among O'Malley's usual clientele.

Daria was in mid-laugh at something one of her friends had said, her head thrown back, exposing the elegant line of her throat. She was older, of course, her face more angular than he remembered, her long black hair now cut into a sleek bob. But her eyes – when they met his, he felt the same jolt he'd experienced on the steps of Topeka High all those years ago.

For a moment, the bar seemed to fade away. It was just the two of them, separated by more than mere physical distance, years of unspoken words and missed opportunities hanging in the air between them. Then Daria's eyes widened in recognition. She offered a small, hesitant smile and a half-wave.

Josh turned back to Mike, his heart pounding. "She saw me," he said, immediately feeling foolish for stating the obvious.

Mike chuckled, shaking his head. "No kidding, Sherlock. Question is, what are you gonna do about it?"

As if on cue, Josh's phone buzzed in his pocket. He pulled it out, nearly dropping it when he saw the name on the screen.

Daria Chen. With trembling fingers, he opened the message:

"Hey stranger. Buy a girl a drink for old times' sake?"

Josh looked up at Mike, who was watching him expectantly. Then he glanced back at Daria, who was pointedly not looking in his direction now, her focus apparently on her friends. He took another swig of his beer, liquid courage burning its way down his throat. As he set the bottle down, his eyes caught on something odd. In the condensation on the dark glass, a pattern seemed to form – intricate swirls that looked eerily like the webbing of his dreamcatcher.

Josh blinked, and the pattern was gone. Just a trick of the light, he told himself. But as he stood, steeling himself to approach Daria's table, he couldn't shake the feeling that something more than a simple reunion was unfolding. In the back of his mind, a voice that sounded suspiciously like his old professor whispered:

"The past is never dead. It's not even past."

Josh squared his shoulders and began to weave through the crowd, unaware that with each step, he was walking into a convergence of past and present that would change his life forever. As he navigated the sea of bodies, memories of Daria washed over him, as vivid and overwhelming as the day they were formed.

Their first date flashed through his mind: a picnic in Gage Park, the autumn leaves a riot of red and gold around them. Daria's laugh as she tried to teach him to use chopsticks, her patience as he fumbled with the unfamiliar utensils. The way the setting sun had caught in her hair, turning it to liquid obsidian.

He remembered lazy Sunday afternoons in his parents' basement, Daria curled against him as they binge-watched documentaries. Her passionate arguments about environmental policy, eyes blazing with conviction. The way she'd challenge him to think bigger, to see beyond the borders of Kansas. But with the sweet memories came the bitter. Their first big fight, sparked by his reluctance to apply to out-of-state colleges. The growing tension as their senior year progressed, Daria's excitement about Columbia a stark contrast to his own uncertainty.

The night before she left for New York replayed in his mind. They'd parked at Lake Shawnee, the water a mirror for the star-studded sky above. Daria had turned to him, her eyes shimmering with unshed tears.

"Come with me," she'd pleaded. "We can figure it out together. New York has community colleges, you could transfer later."

But fear had rooted him to Topeka – fear of the unknown, of failure, of losing the familiar comfort of home. He'd made excuses about family obligations, financial constraints. In the end, he'd watched her go, feeling like he was cutting off a part of himself. Their attempts at long-distance had been painful, filled with stilted video calls and text messages that could never bridge the growing gap between them. Each time Daria spoke of her new life – the vibrancy of New York, her challenging classes, the diverse friends she was making – Josh felt himself shrinking, becoming a relic of a past she was quickly outgrowing.

It was Josh who had finally ended things, in a moment of self-loathing disguised as selflessness. "You deserve someone who can be there with you," he'd said, his voice cracking over the phone. "Someone who shares your dreams."

The memory of Daria's quiet sobs, muffled as if she'd pressed her hand to her mouth, still haunted him. In the years since, he'd tried to convince himself he'd done the right thing. Daria had gone on to thrive, her occasional social media updates painting a picture of the successful life she'd always wanted. Meanwhile, he'd stayed in Topeka, his dreams slowly calcifying into regrets. But now, seeing her again, all the what-ifs came rushing back. What if he'd been braver? What if he'd taken that leap into the unknown with her? Could they have built a life together, supporting each other's ambitions?

As Josh neared Daria's table, a familiar scent wafted past him – a mixture of jasmine and something uniquely her. It transported him instantly to their last embrace at the airport, her tears soaking into his shirt as he memorized her scent, not knowing it would be the last time he'd hold her. The regret hit him anew, a physical ache in his chest. He'd let fear dictate his choices, and in doing so, he might have lost the best thing in his life. Now, as he approached Daria, Josh felt a strange mix of hope and dread. Could this unexpected reunion be a second chance, or would it only serve to remind him of all he'd lost?

He was so lost in his thoughts that he almost didn't notice the shadow that seemed to flicker at the edge of his vision, following his path through the crowd. By the time he registered the movement, he was already at Daria's table, her eyes meeting his with a mixture of warmth and wariness.

"Josh," she said, his name on her lips sending a shiver down his spine. "It's been a long time."

As he opened his mouth to respond, the lights in the bar flickered, plunging them into momentary darkness. In that split second of blackness, Josh could have sworn he felt a cold breath on the back of his neck, carrying a whisper that sounded like old bones rattling together. Then the lights came back on, and Daria was looking at him expectantly, unaware of the shadow that now loomed behind her, its form indistinct but undeniably menacing.

Josh forced a smile, pushing down his unease. "Yeah," he managed, his voice hoarse. "It's good to see you, Daria."

As he sat down, accepting the chair offered by one of Daria's friends, Josh couldn't shake the feeling that this reunion was more than just a chance encounter. Something had been set in motion, something that had been waiting years for this moment.

"So, Josh," Daria said, her smile a mix of warmth and caution, "what have you been up to all these years?"

Josh straightened in his chair, acutely aware of the eyes of Daria's friends on him. "Well, I've been —"

"Let me guess," interrupted a voice from Daria's left. "Still living the dream in Topeka?"

Josh turned to face the speaker, a man with carefully styled hair and a smirk that didn't quite reach his eyes. He wore a crisp button-down that screamed big city professional, a stark contrast to Josh's worn flannel.

"Josh, this is Darren," Daria said, a note of apology in her voice. "We work together at the firm in New York."

"Charmed," Darren said, not sounding charmed at all. "So, Josh, do enlighten us about life in... where are we again?"

"Topeka," Josh replied, fighting to keep his tone neutral. "And actually, I've been working on some interesting projects in Native American history. There's a lot of untold stories right here in Kansas."

He looked at Daria as he spoke, hoping to see a flicker of the interest she used to show in his passion for history. But before she could respond, Darren cut in again.

"Fascinating," he drawled. "I'm sure the thriving metropolis of Topeka is just brimming with cutting-edge historical research. Tell me, do you do your groundbreaking work before or after your shift at... where is it you work, again?"

Josh felt heat rising in his cheeks. "I'm between jobs at the moment, but—"

"Oh, of course," Darren nodded, his voice dripping with faux sympathy. "The job market in Topeka must be so competitive. All those Fortune 500 companies fighting over local talent."

Daria shot Darren a warning look. "That's enough —"

But Darren was on a roll. "You know, Daria here is killing it in environmental law. Just won a huge case against a major polluter. But I'm sure your... what was it? Native American history projects? I'm sure they're equally impactful."

Josh's hands clenched under the table. He opened his mouth, not sure if he was going to defend himself or tell Darren exactly where he could shove his condescension, when a large hand clapped down on his shoulder.

Darren continued in a domineering manner. "I decided to join Daria on our business venture here in...Topeka. You know, kind of a mentoring opportunity. So, you may be seeing a lot of me over these next several weeks."

"There you are, buddy!" Mike's booming voice cut through the tension like a knife. "Been looking all over for you."

Josh looked up gratefully at his friend, who was eyeing the table with a mix of curiosity and concern. "Mike," Josh said, relief evident in his voice. "Uh, you remember Daria?"

Mike's face split into a wide grin. "Of course! Daria, great to see you. And you must be..." he trailed off, looking at Darren.

"Darren," the man supplied, looking slightly put out by the interruption.

"Right, Darren," Mike nodded, not bothering to hide his lack of interest. He turned back to Josh. "Listen, man, I hate to break up the reunion, but I need your help at the bar. That thing we talked about earlier?"

Josh stood quickly, grateful for the escape. "Right, yeah. The thing. Sorry, Daria, I've got to — "

"No worries," Daria said, her eyes darting between Josh and Darren. "Maybe we can catch up later?"

Josh nodded, not trusting himself to speak. As Mike steered him away from the table, he heard Darren's voice fade behind them: "Well, that was quaint. Now, Daria, about the Anderson case..."

Mike guided Josh to the bar, signaling the bartender for two beers. "You okay, man? Looked like you were about to deck that guy."

Josh let out a long breath, the tension slowly leaving his body. "Yeah, I'm fine. Thanks for the save."

"Anytime," Mike said, clapping him on the back. "That's what friends are for, right?"

As the bartender slid their beers across the counter, Josh took a long pull from the bottle, trying to wash away the bitter taste of humiliation. But as he set the beer down, he froze. There, reflected in the mirror behind the bar, was a shadow. It loomed over his shoulder, its form indistinct but unmistakably there. And for a split second, Josh could have sworn he saw red eyes gleaming in its depths, filled with a hunger that made Darren's petty cruelty pale in comparison.

Josh whipped around, heart pounding, but there was nothing there except the usual crowd of O'Malley's patrons. "You sure you're okay?" Mike asked, concern etching his features. "You look like you've seen a ghost."

"Yeah," Josh muttered, turning back to the bar and gripping his beer tightly. "Maybe I have."

As Mike launched into a story about his day at the plant, clearly trying to distract Josh, the shadows in the corners of the bar seemed to deepen. And somewhere in the back of his mind, Josh heard a whisper, as dry as ancient parchment:

"The past feeds on regret, Josh Hawkins. And you're a feast."

Chapter 3
Rekindled Emotions

The harsh glow of Josh's laptop screen illuminated his dimly lit apartment, casting long shadows on the walls. Outside, the streets of Topeka were quiet, the occasional passing car sending fleeting patterns of light across the ceiling. Josh adjusted his webcam, Mike's pixelated face coming into focus on the video chat.

"Alright, man," Mike said, his voice slightly distorted through the speakers. "Operation 'Win Back Daria' is now in session. You sure about this?"

Josh ran a hand through his disheveled hair, acutely aware of the dark circles under his eyes. Sleep had been elusive since the encounter at O'Malley's, his dreams haunted by Daria's smile and... other, less pleasant visions.

"Yeah, I'm sure," Josh replied, trying to inject confidence into his voice. "Seeing her again, Mike... it brought everything back. All the good times, you know?"

Mike's eyebrow raised skeptically. "Uh-huh. And this has nothing to do with Mr. Fancy Pants from New York making you feel bad?"

Josh winced at the memory of Darren's cutting remarks. "It's not about him," he insisted, though a small part of him wondered if that was entirely true. "It's about Daria. About what we had."

He leaned back in his chair, memories washing over him. Daria's laughter echoing through the halls of Topeka High. The way her eyes lit up when she talked about her dreams of changing the world. The soft press of her lips against his prom night, full of promise and possibility.

"We were good together, Mike," Josh said softly. "Really good. And yeah, maybe I screwed it up by not being brave enough to follow her to New York. But now... maybe this is our second chance, you know?"

Mike's face softened on the screen. "I get it, man. But it's been years. You're both different people now. Are you sure you're not just romanticizing the past?"

Josh shook his head vehemently. "No, it's more than that. When I saw her at O'Malley's, it was like... like no time had passed at all. That connection was still there. I could feel it."

He conveniently left out the part about the strange shadows and whispers. No need to make Mike think he was losing it.

"Alright, alright," Mike conceded. "So what's the plan? Please tell me it doesn't involve you showing up outside her window with a boombox."

Josh chuckled, some of the tension easing from his shoulders. "Nothing that drastic. I was thinking of asking her to meet for coffee. You know, somewhere neutral where we can really talk. Catch up properly without... interruptions." The image of Darren's smug face flashed through his mind.

"Not bad," Mike nodded approvingly. "Casual, low pressure. But how are you going to get in touch with her? You got her number last night?"

Josh's face fell. In the chaos of the evening, he'd completely forgotten to ask for Daria's contact information. "Oh, man. No, I didn't."

Mike rolled his eyes. "Amateur hour, Hawkins. Alright, Plan B. Doesn't her family still live in town? Maybe you could —"

Suddenly, Mike's image froze on the screen, his mouth comically half-open. The room plunged into darkness as Josh's laptop abruptly shut off.

"What the hell?" Josh muttered, frantically pressing the power button. Nothing happened. He reached for his phone on the desk, but it too was dead.

In the sudden silence, Josh became acutely aware of his own breathing, quick and shallow in the darkness. The air felt thick, oppressive, as if the shadows themselves had substance.

A soft scratching sound came from the corner of the room. Josh's head snapped towards it, his eyes straining in the blackness. "Hello?" he called out, hating the tremor in his voice.

No response came, but the scratching grew louder, more insistent. It seemed to be coming from the wall where his dreamcatcher hung. Heart pounding, Josh fumbled for the flashlight he kept in his desk drawer. His fingers closed around it just as a new sound filled the room – a low, guttural whisper that seemed to come from everywhere and nowhere at once.

"She is not yours to reclaim, Josh Hawkins. The past is ours. And so are you."

The flashlight clicked on, its beam cutting through the darkness. For a split second, Josh saw something that made his blood run cold – the dreamcatcher on the wall, its intricate web moving and pulsing as if alive, dark shapes writhing within its strands. Then the lights flickered back to life, and everything was normal. The dreamcatcher hung innocently on the wall, still and lifeless. Josh's laptop hummed as it rebooted, Mike's concerned face popping back onto the screen.

"—hear me? Josh! You okay, man? You went dark for a minute there."

Josh turned back to the screen, his face pale, a cold sweat beading on his forehead. "Yeah," he managed, his voice hoarse. "Yeah, I'm fine. Just a... just a power outage."

As Mike launched into a story about the unreliable grid in their neighborhood, Josh's eyes were drawn back to the dreamcatcher. In the soft glow of the desk lamp, he could have sworn he saw a single bead glint red, like a watchful eye. The plans to win Daria back suddenly seemed trivial, overshadowed by a growing sense of dread. Whatever was happening, whatever force seemed to be pushing its way into his life, Josh had a sinking feeling that Daria was somehow at the center of it all.

Josh shook his head, trying to clear the lingering unease. He focused back on Mike, who was still talking about the neighborhood's electrical issues. "Listen, Mike," Josh interrupted, forcing a casual tone, "before I forget, we're still on for that camping trip next weekend, right? Out at Clinton Lake?"

Mike's face brightened. "Hell yeah, we are! I've got the tent and the cooler ready to go. You bringing the fishing gear?"

"You know it," Josh nodded, grateful for the shift to familiar territory. "Maybe we can convince some of the old crew to join us. Like old times."

"Now you're talking," Mike grinned. "Alright, man. I gotta hit the sack. Early shift tomorrow. Don't stay up all night pining over Daria, you hear?"

Josh rolled his eyes but smiled. "Yeah, yeah. Night, Mike."

As the screen went dark, Josh leaned back in his chair, his mind racing. Despite the strange occurrence earlier, he couldn't shake thoughts of Daria from his mind. There had to be a way to reconnect with her, to show her he wasn't the same guy who'd let her go all those years ago.

Suddenly, a memory surfaced. Daria, leaning against her dad's vintage Mustang, talking animatedly about carburetors and engine blocks. She'd always loved old cars, dreaming of restoring one herself someday. Josh sat up straight, an idea forming. What if he could rebuild an old car? It would show Daria he could commit to something, see it through. Plus, it would give them something to talk about, a shared interest to rekindle their connection.

There was just one problem: Josh knew next to nothing about car restoration. But he knew someone who did. Old Willie's junkyard sat on the outskirts of Topeka, a sprawling maze of rusted metal and forgotten dreams.

Willie had been a friend of Josh's grandfather, and he'd always had a soft spot for Josh.

Glancing at the clock, Josh realized it was far too late for a visit now. But first thing tomorrow, he decided, he'd head out to the junkyard and talk to Willie about finding a suitable car to restore. Energized by his new plan, Josh opened his laptop again, this time pulling up websites about classic car restoration. As he scrolled through pages of gleaming chrome and sleek bodywork, he could almost picture himself and Daria working side by side, bringing an old vehicle back to life.

The hours slipped by as Josh fell deeper into his research. It was only when he noticed the first pale light of dawn creeping through his window that he realized he'd been up all night. Rubbing his tired eyes, Josh stood and stretched. As he did, his gaze fell on the dreamcatcher. In the grey morning light, it looked innocent enough, but Josh couldn't shake the memory of what he'd seen – or thought he'd seen – earlier.

Shaking his head, he moved to the kitchen to make some coffee. He had a long day ahead of him, and he needed to be alert when he spoke to Willie. As the coffee brewed, filling the small apartment with its rich aroma, Josh found himself mentally preparing for the conversation. He'd have to convince Willie to not only sell him a car but also to guide him through the restoration process. Josh poured himself a cup of coffee and moved to the window, looking out at the quiet Topeka street below. In the distance, he could just make out the direction of the junkyard. For a moment, he thought he saw a shadow move across the street, more substantial than a mere trick of the light. He blinked, and it was gone.

Sipping his coffee, Josh tried to focus on the task ahead. Find a car. Learn to restore it. Impress Daria. Simple steps, but each fraught with potential pitfalls. And underneath it all, a nagging feeling that he was missing something important, that there was more at stake than just rekindling an old romance. As he finished his coffee and prepared to grab a quick shower before heading to the junkyard, Josh couldn't shake the feeling that his impulsive decision to restore a car was about to set in motion a chain of events that would unearth long-buried secrets, both in the junkyard and in Topeka's hidden history.

Little did he know that at the center of it all, the spirit bound to his dreamcatcher watched and waited, its hunger growing with each passing moment. And as Josh left his apartment, keys in hand and hope in his heart, the shadows seemed to deepen just a little, reaching out with tendrils of darkness that fell just short of his heels. The junkyard awaited, and with it, the next chapter in a story Josh didn't yet realize he was part of.

Chapter 4
A Gem Within the Junk

The gravel crunched under the tires of Josh's beat-up Corolla as he turned onto the long driveway leading to Old Willie's junkyard. As Josh approached the entrance, a cloud of dust erupted in front of him. He slammed on the brakes, heart racing, as a sleek black car emerged from the haze. The car slowed as it passed Josh, and for a moment, he could have sworn he saw the driver looking directly at him. Though he couldn't make out any features through the tinted glass, a chill ran down his spine. There was something... off about the silhouette behind the wheel, something not quite right in its proportions. As quickly as it had appeared, the black car was gone, leaving only a lingering cloud of dust and an uneasy feeling in the pit of Josh's stomach.

Shaking off the strange encounter, Josh pulled up to the small office at the entrance of the junkyard. Old Willie was already outside, his weathered face breaking into a grin as he recognized Josh.

"Well, I'll be," Willie called out as Josh stepped from his car. "If it ain't little Josh Hawkins. Though I reckon I can't call you little anymore, can I?"

Josh smiled, the familiar drawl of Willie's voice helping to dispel some of his unease. "Good to see you, Willie. It's been too long."

"That it has, boy. That it has." Willie's eyes crinkled at the corners as he looked Josh up and down. "Your grandpappy would be proud to see the man you've become. Now, what brings you out to my little slice of paradise?"

As Josh explained his idea about restoring a car, he couldn't help but notice Willie's gaze occasionally flicking to the road behind him, where the black car had disappeared.

"Sounds like quite the project," Willie said when Josh had finished. "You sure you're up for it? Restoring a car ain't for the faint of heart."

Josh nodded, trying to project more confidence than he felt. "I'm sure. I know it'll be a challenge, but... it's important to me."

Willie studied him for a long moment, then nodded. "Alright then. Let's see what we can find for you. But first, tell me something. You happen to notice anything... unusual on your way in?"

Josh hesitated, the image of the black car flashing in his mind. "There was a car leaving as I arrived. Old model, black, looked like it had been restored. Why do you ask?"

Willie's face darkened. "No reason. Just keeping an eye on the comings and goings, you know. Can't be too careful these days." He cleared his throat. "Now, about that car for you. I might have just the thing."

As Willie led him into the maze of junked vehicles, Josh couldn't shake the feeling that the old man wasn't telling him everything. The shadows between the stacks of cars seemed deeper than they should be, and more than once, Josh thought he heard whispers on the wind. They stopped in front of a car covered by a tarp. With a flourish, Willie pulled the cover off, revealing a rusted shell of a 1967 Ford Mustang.

"She ain't much to look at now," Willie said, patting the car's hood affectionately, "but with some work, she could be a real beauty."

Josh circled the car, trying to see past the rust and dents to the potential beneath. As he reached out to touch the driver's side door, a jolt of electricity shot through him. For a split second, the car before him wasn't a rusted wreck, but a gleaming black machine, its engine growling with barely contained power. In the driver's seat sat a figure, too shadowy to make out clearly, but undeniably turning to look at him. Josh jerked his hand back with a gasp. Willie was at his side in an instant, concern etched on his face.

"You alright, boy? You look like you've seen a ghost."

"I'm fine," Josh managed, his heart racing. "Just... surprised myself, I guess."

Willie nodded slowly, his eyes narrowing. "Listen, Josh. There's something you should know about this car. It's got a bit of a... history."

As Willie began to speak, the wind picked up, carrying with it the faint sound of a familiar whisper: "The past is never dead, Josh Hawkins. It's not even past."

Josh shivered, suddenly certain that his impulsive decision to restore a car was about to lead him down a path far darker and more dangerous than he could have imagined. But as he looked at the rusted Mustang, he felt a pull he couldn't explain, a sense that his fate was somehow tied to this vehicle.

"Tell me everything," he said to Willie, his voice steady despite the fear coiling in his gut.

As Willie began his tale, neither of them noticed the raven perched on a nearby stack of crushed cars, its eyes gleaming with an unnatural red light as it watched the exchange with far too much interest for a mere bird.

"Now, son," Willie began, his voice gravelly from years of cigarettes and hard living, "I gotta warn you about this here car. It's got a history, and it ain't pretty."

Josh barely heard the old man's words. His eyes were fixed on the sleek lines of the vintage Mustang, its midnight blue paint still gleaming despite the years of neglect. The price tag dangling from the rearview mirror seemed too good to be true.

Willie continued, his tone growing more urgent. "There's been talk, you know. Folks say this car's been in more accidents than it should've survived. Some even whisper about... fatalities."

A loud caw interrupted Willie's dire warning. Josh glanced up to see a raven perched atop a nearby stack of crushed cars, its beady eyes seeming to stare right through him. The bird's presence sent a chill down his spine, but he quickly shook it off, returning his attention to the car.

"How much did you say it was again?" Josh asked, running his hand along the Mustang's hood, marveling at the coolness of the metal despite the sweltering heat.

Willie sighed, realizing his words were falling on deaf ears. "Listen, boy, I'm trying to tell you —"

"It's perfect," Josh interrupted, a grin spreading across his face. "I want it."

Willie raised an eyebrow, surprised by the young man's eagerness despite his warnings. "Well, if you're set on it, I suppose there's no talking you out of it. But I can't let you drive it out of here today. It needs some work before it's road-worthy."

Josh's excitement dimmed slightly, but he nodded in understanding. "How long will that take?"

"Give me a week," Willie said, scratching his chin thoughtfully. "I'll make sure everything's in order. You can come back next Saturday to pick it up."

"Deal," Josh agreed, extending his hand. As they shook on it, the raven took flight, its wings casting a brief shadow over the car.

"I'll need a deposit to hold it for you," Willie added, eyeing Josh carefully.

Josh fished out his wallet, counting out a portion of the cash. "Here's half. I'll bring the rest when I pick it up next week."

Josh was already imagining himself behind the wheel, the wind in his hair as he cruised down the highway. "I'm sure," he said firmly. "See you in a week, Willie."

Chapter 5
Rust and Revelations

The garage door groaned as Josh rolled it up, revealing the silhouette of his newly acquired treasure. Sunlight spilled into the space, glinting off the midnight blue paint of the vintage 1967 Ford Mustang. A week had passed since he'd driven it home from Old Willie's Auto Salvage, Willie's warnings fading with each mile.

Josh circled the car, running his hand along its cool metal surface. Despite Willie's work to make it "roadworthy," the Mustang was far from its former glory. Rust spots peeked out from under the faded paint, and the interior smelled of musty leather and stale cigarettes.

"Alright, old girl," Josh murmured, patting the hood. "Let's see what we're working with."

He popped the hood, propping it open with a rusty rod. The engine was a mess of grime and corrosion, but Josh could see the potential beneath. He reached for a nearby rag, ready to start cleaning, when something caught his eye. Tucked in the corner of the engine bay was a small, tarnished locket. Josh fished it out, his brow furrowing. The locket was old, its surface etched with intricate swirls. As he turned it over in his hand, a chill ran down his spine.

A sudden caw made him jump. Josh looked up to see a raven perched on the open garage door, its beady eyes fixed on him. It was eerily reminiscent of the bird at the junkyard. Shaking off the unsettling feeling, Josh pocketed the locket and turned back to the task at hand. He'd investigate the mysterious jewelry later. For now, there was work to be done.

Hours slipped by as Josh lost himself in the restoration. He scrubbed away years of grime, replaced corroded hoses, and meticulously documented every part that needed replacing. The work was therapeutic, allowing him to forget the stresses of his day job and the nagging voice in the back of his mind that whispered of the car's dark history. Josh straightened up, wiping sweat from his brow. The engine bay gleamed, a far cry from the rusty mess it had been that morning. He felt a surge of pride at the progress.

Closing the hood, Josh slid into the driver's seat. The key turned in the ignition, and the engine roared to life with a power that belied its age. Josh grinned, revving the engine a few times. But his smile faltered as he caught sight of something in the rearview mirror. For a split second, he could have sworn he saw a figure in the backseat – a young man, his face pale and eyes wide with terror.

Josh whipped around, his heart pounding, but the backseat was empty. He laughed nervously, running a hand through his hair. "Get it together, man," he muttered. "You're letting Willie's ghost stories get to you."

As he shut off the engine, the garage fell into an eerie silence. The locket in his pocket seemed to grow heavier, a tangible reminder of the car's mysterious past. Josh locked up the garage, casting one last glance at the Mustang before heading inside.

Josh couldn't shake the feeling that in restoring this car, he was unearthing more than just old metal and memories. Something darker lurked beneath the surface, something that perhaps should have remained buried in that junkyard.

Josh drifted off to sleep that night, his dreams filled with open roads and the purr of a perfectly tuned engine. Whatever secrets the car held, he was determined to see this restoration through to the end. The 1967 Ford Mustang purred contentedly as Josh guided it along the winding country roads. The restoration had taken months, but as he felt the powerful engine respond to his touch, he knew every long night and skinned knuckle had been worth it.

Golden afternoon sunlight filtered through the trees lining the road, casting dappled shadows across the Mustang's gleaming black hood. Josh smiled, inhaling deeply. The interior still held a faint scent of the original leather, mingled with the crisp pine air freshener he'd hung from the rearview mirror.

As the road straightened out, Josh opened up the throttle. The Mustang surged forward, its engine's roar echoing off the surrounding hills. This was freedom, pure and simple.

The radio crackled to life, startling Josh. He frowned, certain he hadn't turned it on. Through the static, he could just make out the strains of an old doo-wop song. He reached to adjust the dial, but before his fingers touched the knob, the music cleared.

The Platters' "Only You" filled the car, the sound quality impossibly crisp for the old speakers. A movement in his peripheral vision caught Josh's attention. He glanced in the rearview mirror and his heart nearly stopped.

Sitting in the back seat was a young man, no more than twenty. He wore a white T-shirt with the sleeves rolled up, dark jeans, and a red bandana tied loosely around his neck. His hair was slicked back in a perfect 1960s ducktail. The young man stared out the window, a wistful expression on his face. Josh's hands clenched the steering wheel, his knuckles white. He blinked hard, certain he was seeing things. When he looked again, the back seat was empty. Breathing heavily, Josh pulled over to the side of the road. He twisted in his seat, staring into the empty back of the car. There was no sign anyone had been there.

"Get it together, Josh," he muttered to himself, running a shaky hand through his hair.

As he turned back to the front, movement outside the passenger window caught his eye. The same young man stood at the edge of the road, his form flickering like a candle flame in the wind. Their eyes met for a brief moment. The young man's face was a mixture of sadness and urgency, his mouth moving as if trying to speak.

Then, in the blink of an eye, he was gone.

Josh sat there, his heart pounding in his chest. The radio crackled once more and fell silent. The only sound was the steady idle of the Mustang's engine and the blood rushing in his ears.

After several long minutes, Josh put the car in gear and pulled back onto the road. His mind raced with questions. Who was the young man? What was he trying to say? And most importantly, was he somehow connected to the car's mysterious past?

As Josh drove home, considerably slower than before, he couldn't shake the feeling that his restoration project had awakened something long dormant. The Mustang was more than just a classic car — it was a vessel for untold stories, and perhaps, restless spirits.

The sun dipped below the horizon, casting long shadows across the road. In the gathering dusk, Josh found himself glancing more frequently at the rearview mirror, both dreading and hoping to see the ghostly passenger once more.

Josh's hands trembled slightly as he pulled out his cell phone, the memory of his ghostly encounter still fresh in his mind. He needed a dose of normalcy, and who better to provide that than his best friend, Mike? He dialed the familiar number, drumming his fingers on the steering wheel as he waited for an answer.

"Hey, man! What's up?" Mike's cheerful voice came through the speaker.

"Mike, you free tonight?" Josh asked, trying to keep his voice steady. "I was thinking we could meet up. I've got something to show you."

"Ah, man," Mike replied, sounding genuinely disappointed. "I've got a date tonight. Rain check? How about tomorrow?"

Josh felt a pang of disappointment, but quickly pushed it aside. "Yeah, no problem. Tomorrow works. I'll give you a call."

"Let me guess, you finally finished that rust bucket?" Mike chuckled. "Can't wait to see it, man. Talk to you tomorrow!"

After hanging up, Josh sat in silence for a moment, feeling suddenly alone with his thoughts and the looming presence of the Mustang. He needed a distraction, something to ground him in reality. With a decisive nod, he started the engine and headed towards O'Malley's Bar & Grill.

The familiar neon sign buzzed above him as he pulled into the parking lot, making sure to park the Mustang where it was clearly visible from the bar's windows. He couldn't help but smile as he gave it one last admiring glance before heading inside.

The scent of beer and deep-fried food washed over him, along with the sounds of classic rock playing from the jukebox. Josh made his way to the bar, nodding at a few regulars he recognized.

"Well, well," came a gruff voice as Josh settled onto a stool. "If it isn't the car whisperer himself."

Josh looked up to see Pat, the grizzled old bartender, grinning at him. "Hey, Pat. How'd you know it was me?"

Pat jerked his thumb towards the window. "That beauty out there kind of gave you away. That the same heap of rust you've been yammering about for months?"

"The very same," Josh replied, unable to keep the pride from his voice. "Just finished her up today."

Pat let out a low whistle as he slid a cold beer across the bar to Josh. "She's a real stunner, I'll give you that. You know, that reminds me of a car I used to see around here back in the day. Belonged to a young fella named..."

Pat furrowed his brow, trying to remember. "Clint, I think. Clint Perkins."

Josh felt a chill run down his spine. "Clint Perkins?" he repeated, his mouth suddenly dry.

"Yeah, that's it," Pat nodded. "Shame what happened to him. Disappeared one night, him and his girl. Some folks say they drove that car right off Miller's Cliff, but they never found the wreck." He shrugged. "Just an old story, though. Probably nothing to it."

Josh took a long swig of his beer, trying to calm his suddenly racing heart. The story hit too close to home after his earlier experience on the road.

"Say, Pat," Josh began, trying to keep his voice casual. "You wouldn't happen to remember what Clint looked like, would you?"

Pat scratched his chin thoughtfully. "It was a long time ago, but I remember he always wore this red bandana around his neck. Thought he was James Dean or something." He chuckled. "Why do you ask?"

Josh's blood ran cold. The description matched the ghostly figure he'd seen earlier perfectly. "No reason," he managed to say. "Just curious about the local history, you know?"

As the night wore on, Josh nursed his beer, lost in thought. The bar's familiar atmosphere, which usually brought comfort, now felt surreal. He couldn't shake the feeling that in restoring the Mustang, he'd opened a door to something he didn't fully understand.

Josh was lost in thought, absently tracing patterns in the condensation on his beer glass, when the door to O'Malley's swung open with a gust of cool night air. He glanced up, more out of habit than interest, but did a double-take when he recognized the trio entering the bar.

Daria's vibrant dark black hair was unmistakable, even in the dim light of the bar. She was laughing at something Melanie had said, her green eyes sparkling. Beside them, looking somewhat uncomfortable, was Darren, his hands shoved deep in his pockets.

Melanie spotted Josh first, her face lighting up with surprise and delight. "Josh!" she called out, waving enthusiastically. "What are you doing here all by yourself?"

Josh appreciated Melanie's brutal honesty, which she demonstrated early in their friendship while they were both in high school. Before Josh could respond, the three had made their way over to him. Daria gave him a warm hug, while Melanie beamed at him. Darren hung back, shifting his weight from one foot to the other.

"Hey, guys," Josh said, genuinely glad to see them despite his earlier desire for solitude. "Just finished up a project and thought I'd celebrate a bit."

"The car?" Daria asked, her eyes widening. "You finally got it done? That's awesome, Josh!"

Melanie nodded in agreement, then seemed to remember something. She turned to Darren, giving him a pointed look. "Darren," she said, her tone gentle but firm, "isn't there something you wanted to say to Josh?"

The atmosphere suddenly became tense. Josh remembered the argument he'd had with Darren, leading to a heated exchange that had left their friendship strained.

Darren cleared his throat, looking everywhere but at Josh. "Yeah, um," he began, clearly uncomfortable. "Look, Josh, I... I wanted to apologize for what I said about your job situation. It was out of line, and I was wrong."

Josh blinked in surprise. He hadn't expected this.

Melanie nudged Darren gently, encouraging him to continue. "I'm sorry, man."

The sincerity in Darren's voice was unmistakable. Josh felt a weight he hadn't realized he'd been carrying lift from his shoulders. He stood up and extended his hand to Darren. "Thanks, Darren. That means a lot."

Darren shook his hand, relief washing over his face as they shook.

"Alright!" Melanie clapped her hands together, breaking the tension. "Now that that's settled, how about a round of drinks to celebrate Josh's achievement?"

"Sounds great," Josh agreed, feeling a surge of warmth for his friends. "First round's on me."

As Pat came over to take their orders, Daria leaned in, her eyes twinkling with curiosity. "So, Josh, any cool

49

stories about that car of yours? I bet a classic like that has some tales to tell."

Josh hesitated, the memory of his ghostly encounter fresh in his mind. He glanced at his friends' eager faces and made a split-second decision. "You have no idea," he said with a grin. "Let me tell you about this drive I took earlier today..."

As Josh launched into his story, the earlier loneliness dissipated. Whatever mysteries the Mustang held, he realized he didn't have to face them alone. With his friends around him, the supernatural suddenly seemed a little less daunting and a lot more exciting.

The neon sign of O'Malley's cast a red glow over the parking lot as Josh said his goodbyes to Daria, Darren, and Melanie. The night air was cool against his skin, a stark contrast to the warmth of the bar and the company of his friends. Their laughter and theories about his ghostly passenger still echoed in his mind, but now, alone in the darkness, the weight of his earlier encounter settled back onto his shoulders.

Chapter 6
Shadows of the Past

Josh approached his Mustang, its black paint gleaming under the streetlights. He ran his hand along the smooth metal of the hood, a gesture that had become almost ritualistic. "Just you and me again, old girl," he murmured.

As he opened the driver's side door, a flicker of movement caught his eye. Josh froze, his heart suddenly racing. In the reflection on the window, he saw a figure standing behind him – the young man from the 1960s, complete with his white T-shirt, dark jeans, and red bandana.

Josh whirled around, but the parking lot was empty. He let out a shaky breath, trying to calm his nerves. "Get it together," he muttered to himself. "It's just your imagination."

He slid into the driver's seat, the familiar scent of leather and the lingering hint of pine air freshener usually a comfort. But tonight, it felt different – charged somehow, as if the very air inside the car was alive with potential energy. The engine roared to life, its deep rumble grounding Josh in reality. He pulled out of the parking lot, decidedly not looking in the rearview mirror. The streets were nearly empty at this late hour, the yellow lines of the road hypnotic in the Mustang's headlights.

As he drove, Josh found himself taking the long way home, winding through the outskirts of town. The radio crackled to life unprompted, just as it had earlier. This time, the melancholy strains of "Unchained Melody" by The Righteous Brothers filled the car.

"♪ Oh, my love, my darling... ♪"

Josh reached to turn it off, but stopped short. In the passenger seat, barely visible from the corner of his eye, sat the ghostly young man. He was staring straight ahead, his face a mask of sorrow and longing.

"♪ I've hungered for your touch... ♪"

Josh's hands tightened on the steering wheel, his knuckles white. He wanted to look directly at the apparition, but fear kept his eyes locked on the road ahead. "Who are you?" he whispered, his voice barely audible over the music.

The figure turned slowly, fixing Josh with a penetrating gaze. His mouth moved, but no sound came out. Instead, the music swelled:

"♪ Time goes by so slowly... ♪"

Suddenly, the ghostly passenger's eyes widened in terror. He pointed frantically ahead, his silent scream lost in the crescendo of the song. Josh snapped his attention back to the road just in time to see a sharp curve approaching. He yanked the wheel, tires screeching as the Mustang fishtailed dangerously close to the guardrail. Heart pounding, Josh brought the car to a stop on the shoulder. He turned to the passenger seat, but it was empty. The radio had fallen silent, leaving only the sound of his ragged breathing and the tick of the cooling engine.

With shaking hands, Josh pulled out his phone and dialed Mike's number. It rang several times before going to voicemail. "Mike," Josh said, his voice unsteady, "I know it's late, but... something's happening. It's the car. I...I think I need help."

As he ended the call, Josh noticed something on the dashboard that hadn't been there before – a faded photograph. With trembling fingers, he picked it up. In the dim light, he could make out two figures: the young man he'd been seeing, arm in arm with a pretty girl in a 1960s style dress. They were standing in front of an Mustang identical to his, both smiling broadly.

Josh turned the photo over. On the back, in faded ink, was written: "Clint and Sarah, July 4th, 1997."

The chill that ran down Josh's spine had nothing to do with the cool night air. He started the engine again, suddenly eager to get home, away from this lonely stretch of road. But as he pulled back onto the road, he couldn't shake the feeling that his restoration project had become something far more complex – and potentially dangerous – than he'd ever imagined.

The Mustang's headlights cut through the darkness, leading Josh home. But with each mile, the line between past and present, between the living and the dead, seemed to blur a little more.

The harsh sunlight streaming through the half-closed blinds felt like daggers to Josh's eyes as he reluctantly clawed his way back to consciousness. His head throbbed with a dull, insistent pain that seemed to pulse in time with his heartbeat. Groaning, he rolled over, burying his face in the pillow to escape the merciless morning light.

"What the hell happened last night?" he mumbled into the fabric, his voice rough and unfamiliar to his own ears.

Memories came flooding back in disjointed fragments: the bar, his friends, the drive home... and the ghost.

Josh's eyes snapped open, ignoring the protest from his aching head. He sat up too quickly, causing the room to spin around him.

"Whoa," he muttered, steadying himself on the edge of the bed. "Easy does it, Josh."

He glanced around his bedroom, half-expecting to see the spectral figure from the night before lurking in a corner. But there was nothing out of the ordinary - just his usual mess of clothes strewn about and the vintage car posters on the walls. Slowly, carefully, Josh got to his feet. He shuffled out of the bedroom, one hand on the wall for support, the other massaging his temples in a futile attempt to ease the pounding in his skull.

The living room was bathed in the late morning sun. Empty beer bottles from his pre-bar drink stood accusingly on the coffee table. Josh winced at the sight. "No wonder I feel like death warmed over," he muttered.

He made his way to the kitchen, fumbling in the cabinet for aspirin. As he filled a glass with water, his eyes fell on the keys to the Mustang, innocently sitting on the counter where he'd tossed them last night. The sight of them brought a fresh wave of memories - the ghostly passenger, the old photograph, the near-accident on the curve. But in the harsh light of day, with his head pounding and his mouth tasting like old carpet, it all seemed... ridiculous.

"Ghosts," Josh scoffed, swallowing the aspirin. "Yeah, right. And I'm Tupac."

Josh shuffled back to the living room, collapsing onto the couch with a groan. The events of last night seemed like a dream now - or more accurately, a drunken hallucination. He'd had too much to drink, let Pat's story get to him, and then his imagination had run wild on the drive home.

"That's all it was," he told himself firmly. "Just my imagination. And way too much alcohol."

But even as he said it, a nagging doubt persisted in the back of his mind. The ghost had seemed so real, so vivid. And what about the photograph? He couldn't have imagined that, could he?

Josh's eyes darted around the room, searching for the photo he thought he'd brought in with him. But there was no sign of it among the clutter on his coffee table or the mess on his desk.

"Great," he muttered. "Now I'm losing things too."

He leaned back on the couch, closing his eyes against the still-too-bright light. Part of him wanted to go check on the Mustang, to reassure himself that it was just a normal, if exceptionally well-restored car. But the thought of facing the outside world, with its noise and brightness, was too much to bear right now.

"Later," he promised himself. "I'll deal with it all later."

As he drifted off into a fitful doze, Josh couldn't shake the feeling that he was missing something important. But for now, the pounding in his head drowned out the whispers of doubt, and the mysteries of the night before faded into the haze of his hangover.

In the quiet of his apartment, the line between reality and imagination blurred, leaving Josh teetering on the edge of belief and skepticism. The truth, whatever it might be, would have to wait for a clearer head and a stronger stomach. A thunderous pounding on the front door jolted Josh awake. He bolted upright on the couch, instantly regretting the sudden movement as his head throbbed in protest. The pounding continued, each knock feeling like a hammer blow to his fragile skull.

"Josh! Come on, man, open up!" Mike's voice, muffled but unmistakable, came through the door.

Josh stumbled to his feet, confusion written across his face. "Mike?" he called out, his voice still rough from sleep. "What's going on?"

He fumbled with the lock and swung the door open to reveal Mike, dressed in hiking boots and cargo shorts, a look of exasperation on his face.

"Dude, seriously?" Mike said, taking in Josh's disheveled appearance. "Don't tell me you forgot."

Josh blinked, his brain struggling to catch up. "Forgot what?"

Mike pushed past him into the apartment, shaking his head. "Our camping trip, man! We've been planning this for weeks. Two days in the great outdoors, remember?"

The realization hit Josh like a bucket of cold water. The camping trip. Of course. How could he have forgotten?

"Oh, man," Josh muttered, running a hand through his messy hair. "Mike, I'm so sorry. I... I had a weird night."

Mike's expression softened slightly. "Yeah, I got your voicemail. Sounded like you tied one on pretty good. You okay?"

The events of the previous night came flooding back - the ghost, the near-accident, the photograph. Josh opened his mouth to explain, then closed it again. How could he possibly describe what had happened without sounding crazy?

"I'm fine," he said finally. "Just... yeah, too much to drink. Give me ten minutes to pack?"

Mike nodded, glancing around the cluttered apartment. "Sure, but make it quick. We're already behind schedule."

Josh hurried to his bedroom, throwing clothes and camping gear into a duffel bag. As he packed, he couldn't shake the feeling that he was forgetting something important. The Mustang sat in the parking lot, a tangible link to the mysteries of the night before. Part of him wanted to stay, to investigate further, to prove to himself that it had all been real.

But another part, a part that was growing louder by the minute, welcomed the chance to get away. To put some distance between himself and the car, between reality and whatever twilight zone he'd stumbled into last night.

"Ready!" Josh announced, emerging from his room with his hastily packed bag.

Mike, who had been flipping through a car magazine he'd found on the coffee table, stood up. "Great. My car's out front. You good to go?"

Josh hesitated for a moment, his eyes darting to the Mustang's keys on the kitchen counter. "Yeah," he said finally. "Let's take your car. I think... I think I could use a break from driving for a bit."

As they headed out, Josh cast one last glance at his apartment. The Mustang's keys glinted in the sunlight streaming through the window, almost as if they were watching him leave.

"You sure you're okay?" Mike asked as they climbed into his practical, decidedly non-haunted sedan.

Josh forced a smile. "Yeah, just tired. Nothing a couple days in the woods won't fix, right?"

As Mike's car pulled away from the curb, Josh watched his apartment building recede in the side mirror. The Mustang, barely visible in the parking lot, seemed to shimmer slightly in the heat haze rising from the asphalt.

For a moment, just before it disappeared from view, Josh could have sworn he saw a figure standing next to it - a young man in a white T-shirt and red bandana. But then Mike turned a corner, and the image was gone.

Josh leaned back in his seat, closing his eyes. Two days in the wilderness. Two days away from the car, away from ghostly apparitions and impossible photographs. Two days to clear his head and convince himself that it had all been a product of an overactive imagination and too much alcohol.

Josh felt the tension begin to ease from his shoulders. Whatever was going on with the Mustang, whatever mysteries were waiting to be unraveled, they could wait. For now, he was just a guy on a camping trip with his best friend, leaving the real world behind.

Or so he hoped.

Chapter 7
Joyride

Darren hunched down in his rental Honda Civic, parked just out of sight down the street from Josh's apartment. He watched as Josh, looking worse for wear, stumbled out of his building with Mike.

A twinge of jealousy twisted in Darren's gut as he observed their easy camaraderie, the way Mike clapped Josh on the back as they loaded camping gear into Mike's car. "Must be nice," Darren muttered to himself, "having all the time in the world for little adventures."

As Mike's car pulled away, Darren's eyes were drawn to the gleaming black 1967 Ford Mustang sitting in the parking lot. The morning sun glinted off its immaculate paint job, and even from a distance, Darren could appreciate the car's classic lines and powerful presence.

Darren remembered the previous night at O'Malley's, how he'd swallowed his pride and apologized to Josh. The memory left a bitter taste in his mouth. Sure, the car looked great, but what was the point of pouring all that time and money into something if you weren't even going to drive it?

An idea began to form in Darren's mind, reckless and tempting. Josh would be gone for days. The Mustang was just sitting there, begging to be driven. Darren's fingers twitched on the steering wheel of his own shabby car.

"It would serve him right," Darren reasoned, his voice barely a whisper in the empty car. "Just a quick spin. He'd never even know."

Before he could talk himself out of it, Darren was out of his car and walking casually towards Josh's apartment building. He glanced around, but the street was deserted in the late morning lull. His heart pounded as he approached the Mustang, its black paint seeming to absorb the sunlight.

Darren ran a hand along the car's flank, marveling at the smooth, cool metal beneath his fingers. He tried the driver's side door, hardly daring to hope – and to his surprise, it opened. Josh must have forgotten to lock it in his hungover rush.

"It's a sign," Darren murmured, sliding into the driver's seat. The rich scent of leather enveloped him, mingled with a faint, unfamiliar cologne that made him wrinkle his nose. He gripped the steering wheel, feeling the thrill of anticipation course through him.

Now for the real test. Darren leaned down, fumbling under the steering column. He'd learned a thing or two about hot-wiring cars in his misspent youth, a skill he wasn't particularly proud of but had never quite forgotten. After a few tense minutes, the Mustang's engine roared to life.

Darren sat up, a wide grin spreading across his face. "Oh, baby," he breathed, revving the engine. The deep, powerful rumble sent shivers down his spine.

He put the car in gear and eased out of the parking spot, trying to look as natural as possible. As he pulled onto the street, Darren felt a rush of exhilaration. He'd done it. He was actually driving Josh's prized Mustang.

As Darren accelerated, heading for the open road outside of town, the radio suddenly crackled to life. The opening notes of "Bad Moon Rising" by Creedence Clearwater Revival filled the car.

"♪ I see a bad moon rising... ♪"

"Hell yeah," Darren grinned, turning up the volume. "Now it's a party."

Darren rolled down the windows, letting the wind whip through his hair as he pushed the Mustang faster. The thrill of speed, the power of the engine, the forbidden nature of his joyride – it was intoxicating.

The neon sign of O'Malley's Bar buzzed faintly, casting a red glow over Daria and Melanie as they stood on the sidewalk. The night air was crisp, carrying the faint scent of cigarette smoke and spilled beer from the bar's open door.

"I can't believe Darren stood us up," Daria grumbled, checking her phone for the hundredth time. "He's the one who insisted on meeting here."

Melanie shrugged, her eyes scanning the nearly empty street. "Maybe something came up. You know how he gets, unreliable really."

As if on cue, the rumble of a powerful engine cut through the quiet night. Both women turned their heads toward the sound, watching as a sleek black Mustang rolled into view under the yellow glow of a streetlight.

"Wait...there's Josh..." Daria started, but her words trailed off as the car drew closer. Her brow furrowed in confusion. "Wait a second. That's not Josh driving."

Melanie squinted, then gasped. "Is that a Ford Mustang?"

Daria nodded in affirmation. "It's Darren! What's he doing in Josh's car?"

The Mustang slowed as it approached the intersection near the bar, giving the women a clear view inside.

Darren sat behind the wheel, his face a mask of tension even in the dim light. But it was what — or rather, who — they saw in the backseat that made their blood run cold.

A figure sat there, barely visible in the shadows. It was a man, or at least the shape of one, dressed in what looked like an old-fashioned 60s biker. But there was something... off about him. His edges seemed blurred, as if he wasn't quite solid.

"Do you see that?" Melanie whispered, gripping Daria's arm. "In the backseat?"

Daria nodded slowly, her eyes wide. "Who is that? I've never seen him before."

Melanie had an intense stare as well, noticeably more disturbed than her friend.

As they watched, the figure in the backseat turned, seeming to look directly at them. For a split second, the streetlight illuminated its face — or what should have been a face. Instead, they saw a void, a swirling darkness where features should have been.

Both women recoiled instinctively. By the time they looked back, the Mustang was already moving past them, picking up speed as it disappeared down the street.

"What the hell was that?" Daria breathed, her voice shaky.

Melanie shook her head, still staring after the vanished car. "I don't know, but something's very wrong. Why is Darren driving Josh's car?"

They stood in stunned silence for a moment, the chill of the night suddenly feeling much colder. Finally, Daria pulled out her phone again.

"I'm calling Josh," she said firmly. "He needs to know about this. And then we're going to find out what's going on with Darren."

As Daria dialed, Melanie couldn't shake the image of that faceless figure from her mind. She had a sinking feeling that they had just witnessed the beginning of something terrifying — something that reached far beyond a borrowed car and a mysterious passenger.

Darren took a sharp turn onto a quieter country road, catching a glimpse of something in the rearview mirror that made his blood run cold. For just a moment, he could have sworn he saw a young man in the back seat, dressed in clothes from another era, staring at him with a mixture of anger and sorrow.

Darren's head whipped around, but the back seat was empty. He turned back to the road, his hands shaking slightly on the wheel.

"Get it together, man," he muttered to himself. "It's just your imagination."

But as he drove on, the exhilaration of the joyride began to fade, replaced by an growing sense of unease. The music from the radio seemed to take on a menacing tone, and the shadows on the road ahead seemed to flicker and dance at the edges of his vision.

Darren pressed down harder on the accelerator, as if he could outrun the creeping dread that was settling over him. But with every mile, every turn of the winding country road, he couldn't shake the feeling that he wasn't alone in the car – and that whatever was with him was far from happy about his impulsive theft.

The Mustang roared down the empty road, carrying Darren deeper into an adventure he hadn't bargained for, with consequences he couldn't begin to imagine.

Darren's knuckles whitened as he gripped the steering wheel of his '67 Mustang. The desert highway stretched endlessly before him, a ribbon of asphalt cutting through the arid landscape. The sun had long since dipped below the horizon, leaving only the faint glow of his headlights to illuminate the road ahead.

He'd been driving for hours, the monotony of the journey broken only by the occasional rustle of the map on the passenger seat. That's when he first noticed it – a flicker in his peripheral vision, like a shadow passing over the rearview mirror.

Darren's eyes flicked up, meeting nothing but the empty backseat. He shook his head, chalking it up to fatigue. But as the miles ticked by, the sensation grew stronger. The air in the car seemed to thicken, pressing down on him with an almost tangible weight.

Static hissed through the speakers, occasionally broken by snatches of music—old tunes from the '60s that Darren vaguely recognized. He reached out to turn it off, but his hand froze midway.

In the passenger seat sat a man.

Darren's heart lurched in his chest. The figure was translucent, flickering like an old television set struggling to hold its picture. It—he—wore faded jeans, a white t-shirt, and had slicked back black hair. His face was gaunt, eyes sunken and lifeless, fixed on some point in the distance.

"Jesus Christ!" Darren yelped, the car swerving wildly before he regained control.

The ghost—because what else could it be?—turned slowly to face him. Its mouth opened, but instead of words, a low, guttural moan filled the car. The sound raised goosebumps on Darren's arms and sent a chill racing down his spine.

"Who... what are you?" Darren stammered, his voice barely above a whisper.

The apparition's form flickered more violently now, its features distorting grotesquely. One moment, it was the dapper businessman, the next, a horrifying visage of decay and rot. The moaning grew louder, drowning out the static from the radio.

Darren's foot pressed harder on the accelerator, the needle climbing past 80, 90, 100 mph. The ghost matched his panic, its movements becoming more erratic. It phased in and out of existence, appearing in the backseat one second, then directly in front of Darren the next.

Darren took a brief moment to pray, thinking that at any moment his end would come.

The temperature in the car plummeted. Darren's breath came out in visible puffs as he wrestled with the steering wheel. The ghost's wailing reached a fever pitch, and suddenly, ice began to form on the windshield.

"Get out!" Darren screamed, though whether he was addressing the spirit or himself, he wasn't sure.

The Mustang fishtailed as Darren fought to maintain control. Through the rapidly frosting windshield, he caught sight of a sharp bend in the road ahead. He pumped the brakes, but the pedal went straight to the floor with no resistance.

The ghost lunged at him, its skeletal hands reaching for Darren's throat. He threw his arms up in defense, losing his grip on the wheel. The last thing he saw was the guardrail rushing towards him, the ghost's unearthly scream mingling with the screech of tearing metal as the world turned upside down.

And then there was silence.

Chapter 8
Whispers in the Woods

The sun hung low on the horizon, painting the sky in hues of orange and purple as Josh's pickup truck rumbled down the dirt road leading into Lake Shawnee. Beside him, Mike fiddled with the radio, trying to catch a clear signal.

"Man, I can't believe you left your precious Mustang behind for this trip," Mike chuckled, giving up on the radio and leaning back in his seat.

Josh shrugged, his eyes scanning the deepening shadows between the trees. "Darren needed it for something. Besides, this old truck is better for hauling our gear."

As they rounded a bend, the lake came into view, its surface a mirror reflecting the twilight sky. Josh pulled into a small clearing near the water's edge and cut the engine.

"Home sweet home for the next couple of days," he announced, hopping out of the truck.

The two friends worked quickly to set up camp, the familiar routine requiring little discussion. Josh wrestled with the tent poles while Mike unpacked their supplies. The forest around them grew quieter as night fell, the daytime chorus of birds giving way to the occasional hoot of an owl and the persistent chirping of crickets.

"Hey, you hear about the history of this place?" Mike asked as he hammered the last tent stake into the ground.

Josh paused, a bundle of firewood in his arms. "What do you mean?"

Mike's voice dropped to a conspiratorial whisper. "They say this lake is haunted. Apparently, it was built on an old Native American burial ground. There have been a bunch of accidents and drownings over the years."

"Come on, man," Josh scoffed, arranging the wood for their fire. "You know I have a degree in that stuff."

But as he spoke, a chill ran down his spine that had nothing to do with the cooling night air. He couldn't shake the feeling that they were being watched.

Mike shrugged, pulling out his lighter. "I'm just saying, maybe we should've picked a different spot."

The fire sparked to life, pushing back the encroaching darkness. Both men sat back, enjoying the warmth and the hypnotic dance of the flames. For a while, they chatted about nothing in particular – work, relationships, plans for the future.

As the night wore on, a mist began to creep across the lake's surface. Josh found his eyes drawn to it, watching as it thickened and began to creep towards the shore. There was something unnatural about its movement, almost purposeful.

"Hey, Mike," he started, his voice hesitant. "Does that mist seem weird to you?"

But Mike didn't answer. Josh turned to find his friend staring intently into the woods behind them, his face pale in the firelight.

"What's wrong?" Josh asked, dread pooling in his stomach.

Mike swallowed hard. "I thought I saw something. A figure, standing between the trees. But it was... wrong somehow. Like it wasn't all there."

Josh was about to respond when a twig snapped in the darkness beyond their campsite. Both men jumped, instinctively moving closer to the fire.

"Probably just an animal," Josh said, trying to convince himself as much as Mike.

But deep down, he knew that whatever was out there in the shadows was no ordinary forest creature. As the mist continued to creep closer and unseen eyes watched from the darkness, Josh couldn't help but wonder if they had made a terrible mistake in coming to Lake Shawnee.

The crackling of the fire filled the uneasy silence that had fallen between Josh and Mike. Josh poked at the embers with a stick, his mind clearly elsewhere. Finally, he took a deep breath and turned to his friend.

"Look, Mike, there's something I need to tell you," Josh said, his voice low and serious. "It's about my car - the Mustang."

Mike raised an eyebrow. "What about it? Did you break it or something?"

Josh shook his head. "No, it's not that. It's... well, it's going to sound crazy."

"Crazier than haunted lakes?" Mike chuckled, but his smile faded when he saw the grave expression on Josh's face.

"A few days ago, I started seeing something - someone - in my car," Josh continued, his eyes fixed on the dancing flames. "It's a man, dressed like he's straight out of the '60s. Jeans, T-shirt, slicked back hairdo. But here's the thing - he just appears out of nowhere. One minute the car's empty, the next, he's there."

Mike leaned forward, his brow furrowed. "What do you mean, 'appears'?"

"I mean, he literally materializes. Like a... like a ghost." Josh's voice dropped to almost a whisper on the last word. "And he doesn't just sit there. He watches me, follows me with his eyes. Sometimes, I swear I can feel him even when I can't see him."

A tense silence fell between them, broken only by the pop and hiss of the fire. Mike's expression was a mix of concern and disbelief.

"Josh, buddy," Mike started cautiously, "have you been under a lot of stress lately? I know that guy Darren's been giving you a hard time."

Josh's head snapped up. "You think I'm imagining this?"

Mike held up his hands placatingly. "I'm not saying that. But you gotta admit, it sounds pretty far-fetched. Maybe it's just your mind playing tricks on you. Adrenaline can do weird things, especially when you're dealing with a bully like Darren."

"I know what I saw," Josh insisted, his voice rising slightly. "This isn't stress or tricks of the light or whatever. There's something in my car, Mike. Something that shouldn't be there."

Mike sighed, reaching out to pat Josh's shoulder. "Look, I believe that you believe it. But ghosts? In your car? There's got to be a more logical explanation."

Josh opened his mouth to argue further but was cut off by a sudden gust of wind that swept through their campsite, causing the fire to flare and sending sparks swirling into the night sky. Both men instinctively huddled closer to the fire, their eyes scanning the darkness beyond.

"Did you feel that?" Josh whispered, a tremor in his voice.

Mike nodded slowly, his earlier skepticism giving way to unease. "Yeah, I did."

As they sat there, the strange mist from the lake continued to creep closer, tendrils of fog curling around their feet. The feeling of being watched intensified, and Josh couldn't shake the terrifying thought that somehow, impossibly, the presence from his car had followed him here.

"Maybe," Mike said softly, his eyes wide as he stared into the mist-shrouded woods, "maybe we should invite this ghost of yours on our next camping. trip!"

The first rays of sunlight filtered through the trees, casting long shadows across the campsite. Josh unzipped the tent flap, squinting as he emerged into the crisp morning air. The events of the previous night felt distant in the soft glow of dawn, almost like a half-remembered dream.

Mike was already up, crouched by the remnants of last night's fire, coaxing it back to life. A battered coffee pot sat nearby, ready to be put to use.

"Morning," Mike called out, his voice still rough with sleep. "Sleep okay?"

Josh shrugged, running a hand through his disheveled hair. "As well as you can on the ground, I guess."

He made his way over to the fire, gratefully accepting the mug of coffee Mike handed him. For a while, they sat in companionable silence, sipping the hot brew and watching as the mist on the lake slowly dissipated in the growing light.

"So," Mike finally said, "about last night..."

Josh tensed, anticipating another round of skepticism about his ghostly passenger. But Mike surprised him.

"I've been thinking about what you said. About the guy in your car. I'm not saying I believe in ghosts, but... well, weird stuff happens sometimes, right?"

Josh nodded slowly, a weight he hadn't realized he'd been carrying lifting slightly from his shoulders. "Yeah, it does. Thanks, Mike."

They lapsed back into silence, finishing their coffee as the forest around them came to life with birdsong and the rustling of small animals.

"Guess we should start packing up," Mike said eventually, standing and stretching. "Got a long drive ahead of us."

Josh didn't respond immediately. He was staring out at the lake, a frown creasing his brow.

"Josh? You okay, man?"

Josh blinked, turning back to his friend. "Yeah, I just... I've got this weird feeling."

Mike raised an eyebrow. "Weird how?"

"I can't really explain it," Josh said, shaking his head. "It's like... you know that feeling you get when you've forgotten something important? But worse. Like something bad has happened, but I don't know what."

Mike's expression grew concerned. "Bad how? You think it's related to... you know, your car situation?"

Josh shrugged helplessly. "I don't know. Maybe. It's just this sense of... dread, I guess. Like something's gone wrong."

Mike was quiet for a moment, then clapped Josh on the shoulder. "Look, why don't we pack up and head back?"

Josh nodded, grateful for the suggestion. As they began breaking down the campsite, he couldn't shake the nagging feeling in the pit of his stomach. The peaceful morning suddenly felt like the calm before a storm, and Josh couldn't help but wonder what was waiting for them back in town.

As he rolled up his sleeping bag, a glint of something metallic caught his eye near the edge of the campsite. Curious, he walked over and bent down to examine it. His blood ran cold as he recognized what it was – a small, silver tie clip, its style unmistakably from the 1960s.

Josh straightened up quickly, his eyes darting around the campsite. But there was nothing out of the ordinary to be seen. Just trees, the lake, and Mike packing up the tent, unaware of Josh's discovery.

With a shaking hand, Josh pocketed the tie clip. Whatever was happening, whatever had followed him here, he was now certain of one thing – it wasn't over. Not by a long shot.

Mike's sedan rumbled down the highway, leaving the tranquil shores of Lake Shawnee behind. Josh sat behind the wheel, his knuckles white as he gripped it tightly. The tie clip he'd found at the campsite felt like it was burning a hole in his pocket, a constant reminder of the inexplicable events of the past few days.

Mike fiddled with the radio, trying to find a station that wasn't mostly static. "Man, the reception out here is terrible," he grumbled.

Josh barely heard him, his mind racing with possibilities. Should he tell Mike about the tie clip? Would his friend finally believe him, or would he come up with another rational explanation?

Suddenly, the static cleared, and a voice came through the speakers:

"...breaking news from Topeka. Local authorities have reported a disturbing discovery in an industrial park just outside the city limits."

Both men perked up, exchanging a quick glance before turning their attention back to the radio.

The reporter continued, her voice grave: "The body of an unidentified individual was found in a parking lot early this morning. While details are still emerging, police have confirmed that the death is being treated as suspicious."

Josh felt his stomach drop. The feeling of dread that had been gnawing at him all morning intensified.

"Witnesses report seeing a black classic car, possibly a Ford Mustang, leaving the scene shortly before the body was discovered. Police are urging anyone with information to come forward."

The blood drained from Josh's face. He pulled the sedan over to the shoulder of the road, his hands shaking as he put it in park.

"Josh?" Mike's voice was filled with concern. "You okay, man? You look like you've seen a ghost."

Josh let out a humorless laugh. "Maybe I have," he muttered.

"What are you talking about?"

Josh took a deep breath, then reached into his pocket and pulled out the tie clip. "I found this at our campsite this morning," he said, holding it out for Mike to see. "It's from the '60s, Mike. Just like the ghost in my car."

Mike stared at the small silver object, his earlier skepticism visibly crumbling. "But... how?"

"I don't know," Josh said, shaking his head. "But I think... I think it followed us to the lake. And now this news about a body found near an Mustang..." His voice trailed off, the implications too terrifying to voice.

Mike was quiet for a long moment, processing everything. Finally, he spoke, his voice barely above a whisper. "What do we do now?"

Josh started the sedan again, pulling back onto the road with grim determination but unable to answer. As they sped towards Topeka, the tie clip sat between them on the dashboard, a silent reminder of the supernatural force they were up against. The peaceful camping trip now felt like a distant memory, replaced by a growing sense of dread and the realization that their brush with the unexplained was far from over.

Chapter 9
Accusations

The sun was dipping below the horizon, painting the sky in hues of orange and purple, as Mike's sedan pulled into his driveway. The camping gear rattled in the back, a reminder of the trip that now felt like it had happened a lifetime ago. Both Josh and Mike were silent, the weight of the news report and their speculations hanging heavy between them.

As Mike cut the engine, he noticed something out of place. A police cruiser was parked across the street, its presence ominous in the quiet suburban setting.

"What the hell?" Mike muttered, following Josh's gaze.

Before either of them could say anything more, the cruiser's door opened, and a figure stepped out. In the fading light, they could make out the unmistakable silhouette of a sheriff's deputy, complete with a wide-brimmed hat.

83

Josh's heart began to race. "Stay cool," he whispered to Mike, more to steady himself than his friend. "Let's just see what this is about."

They exited the sedan, the gravel crunching under their feet seeming unnaturally loud in the tense atmosphere. The deputy approached, his face unreadable in the shadows cast by his hat.

"Joshua Hawkins?" the deputy asked, his voice gruff and businesslike.

Josh nodded, trying to keep his voice steady. "That's me. Is there a problem, officer?"

The deputy's hand moved to rest on his belt, close to his handcuffs. "I'm Deputy Garcia with the Shawnee County Sheriff's Office. I need you to confirm something for me. Are you the owner of a black 1967 Ford Mustang, license plate KAZ 2Y5?"

Josh's mouth went dry. He could feel Mike tense beside him. "Yes," he managed to say. "That's my car. But I lent it to a friend a couple of days ago. Is something wrong?"

Deputy Garcia's expression hardened. "Mr. Hawkins, I'm going to need you to turn around and place your hands behind your back."

"What? Why?" Josh's voice rose in panic. "I haven't done anything!"

"Josh," Mike started to interject, but the deputy cut him off with a sharp look.

"Sir, please step back," Garcia ordered Mike before turning back to Josh. "Mr. Hawkins, you are under detention as a suspect in the murder of Darren Kovacs. You have the right to remain silent. Anything you say can and will be used against you in a court of law."

The world seemed to tilt on its axis as Deputy Garcia continued reading Josh his Miranda rights. The words "murder" and "Darren" echoed in his head, drowning out everything else. He felt the cold metal of handcuffs close around his wrists, the reality of the situation crashing down on him.

"This has to be a mistake," Mike was saying, his voice sounding distant to Josh's ears. "We've been camping, we just got back. Josh couldn't have —"

"Sir, I won't tell you again to step back," Deputy Garcia warned. "Your friend will have a chance to explain himself down at the station. For now, I need you to stay out of this."

As Josh was led to the cruiser, his mind raced. Darren was dead? Murdered? And they thought he had done it? The ghost, the tie clip, the news report – it all swirled together in a dizzying vortex of confusion and fear.

Just before Garcia helped him into the back of the cruiser, Josh caught sight of something that made his blood run cold. There, across the street, partially hidden behind a tree, stood a figure in a 1960s biker outfit. Even in the deepening twilight, Josh could see that where its face should be, there was only a swirling darkness.

Then the car door slammed shut, and the figure vanished, leaving Josh to wonder if he had imagined it. As the cruiser pulled away, Josh watched his house, Mike, and his normal life recede in the rear-view mirror. He couldn't shake the feeling that he was being pulled into something far darker and more dangerous than a simple murder investigation.

Whatever was happening, Josh realized with a chill, it was far from over. In fact, it felt like it was just beginning.

The fluorescent lights of the police station buzzed overhead, harsh and unforgiving. Josh felt numb as he was led through the processing procedures – fingerprints, mugshot, personal effects catalogued and stored away. Each step felt like another nail in a coffin he couldn't quite believe he was in.

"This way," a uniformed officer grunted, guiding Josh down a sterile hallway. They stopped at a nondescript door, and the officer ushered him inside.

The interrogation room was small and sparse – a metal table, three chairs, and a large mirror that Josh knew was likely a two-way observation window. The officer directed him to sit, then left without a word, the lock clicking ominously behind him.

Josh stared at his reflection in the mirror, barely recognizing the haggard, frightened face that looked back at him. How had everything gone so wrong so quickly? His mind raced, trying to piece together the events of the past few days. The ghost, the camping trip... Darren. Dead. Murdered.

He didn't know how long he sat there, lost in his thoughts, before the door opened again. A man in a rumpled suit entered, a thick file tucked under his arm. He had the weary look of someone who had seen too much and slept too little.

"Mr. Hawkins," the man said, settling into the chair across from Josh. "I'm Detective Reeves. I'd like to ask you a few questions about your whereabouts over the past 48 hours."

Josh swallowed hard. "Look, Detective, there's been a huge mistake. I didn't kill Darren. I've been camping with my friend Mike. We just got back when your deputy picked me up."

Reeves raised an eyebrow, jotting something in his notepad. "Camping, huh? Convenient timing. And this friend of yours, he'll corroborate your story?"

"Of course he will," Josh said, a hint of desperation creeping into his voice. "Because it's the truth. Call him, please. His name is Michael Harris."

The detective made another note, then fixed Josh with a penetrating stare. "Mr. Hawkins, can you explain to me why your car was found at the scene of Mr. Kovacs' murder?"

"Mm-hmm," Reeves hummed noncommittally. "And when was the last time you saw Mr. Kovacs?"

Detective Reeves seemed to sense his internal struggle. "Is there something else you want to tell me, Mr. Hawkins? Now would be the time to come clean."

Josh took a deep breath. "Detective, what I'm about to say is going to sound... well, crazy. But I swear it's the truth."

Reeves leaned back in his chair, his expression unreadable. "Go on."

"For the past week or so, I've been seeing something – someone – in my car. A man, dressed like he's from the 1960s. At first, I thought I was imagining things, but..." Josh trailed off, then reached into his pocket, producing the silver tie clip. "I found this at our campsite this morning. It's from the '60s, just like the ghost."

The detective's eyes narrowed as he examined the tie clip. "A ghost? Mr. Hawkins, are you saying a ghost killed Darren Kovacs?"

Put that way, it sounded ridiculous. Josh slumped in his chair. "I don't know what I'm saying, Detective. I just know that something strange is going on, and Darren's death is somehow connected to it."

Reeves was quiet for a long moment, studying Josh intently. Finally, he stood up. "I think we're done for now, Mr. Hawkins. An officer will escort you to a holding cell. I strongly suggest you think very carefully about the story you want to stick with."

As the detective reached for the door, Josh called out, "Wait! Please, just... check the security cameras at the industrial park. You'll see I wasn't there."

Reeves paused, hand on the doorknob. Without turning around, he said, "That's the thing, Mr. Hawkins. We did check the cameras. They show your car arriving and leaving... but the driver's face is never clearly visible." He looked back at Josh, his expression grim. "It's almost like they knew exactly where the blind spots were."

With that, he left, leaving Josh alone with the weight of his words. As the reality of his situation sank in, Josh couldn't shake the feeling that he was caught in the middle of something far more sinister than a simple murder investigation. Something that defied logical explanation.

Detective Reeves had just reached for the door handle when a sharp knock interrupted them. He turned, eyebrow raised, as a young officer poked his head into the room.

"Sorry to interrupt, Detective," the officer said, slightly out of breath. "But we've got a situation at the front desk you need to know about."

Reeves frowned. "Can't it wait? I'm in the middle of an interrogation here."

The officer shook his head. "I don't think so, sir. There are three people out there insisting they need to speak with you immediately. They're saying they can corroborate this man's alibi." He nodded towards Josh.

Josh's heart leapt. Could it be Mike? But who were the other two?

Detective Reeves' frown deepened. He turned back to Josh, studying him with renewed interest. "You expecting company, Mr. Hawkins?"

Josh shook his head, genuinely confused. "No, I... I mean, I told you to call my friend Mike, but I don't know about anyone else."

Reeves seemed to consider for a moment, then nodded to the officer. "Alright, bring them to Interview Room B. I'll be there in a minute." As the officer left, Reeves fixed Josh with a stern look. "Sit tight, Mr. Hawkins. We're not done here."

With that, he strode out of the room, leaving Josh alone once again. But now, instead of despair, Josh felt a flicker of hope. Someone was here to help him. But who?

Several agonizing minutes passed before the door opened again. This time, a different officer entered. "On your feet, Hawkins. Detective wants you in Interview Room B."

Confused but compliant, Josh followed the officer down the hallway. As they approached a door marked "Interview Room B," he could hear muffled voices from inside. The officer opened the door, and Josh stepped in, unprepared for the sight that greeted him.

Seated at a large table were Mike, looking worried but determined, and two women Josh recognized with a jolt: Daria and Melanie, the girls they were supposed to meet at O'Malley's Bar the night Darren died. Detective Reeves stood at the head of the table, his arms crossed, wearing an expression of barely concealed frustration.

"Josh!" Mike exclaimed, half-rising from his chair before the detective motioned for him to sit back down.

"Mr. Hawkins," Reeves said, gesturing to an empty chair. "Please, join us. It seems these folks have quite a story to tell."

As Josh took his seat, Daria spoke up, her voice firm. "Detective, we've been trying to tell you. Josh couldn't have killed anyone. We saw him – well, we saw his car – the night Darren died."

Melanie nodded vigorously. "That's right. We were outside O'Malley's, waiting for Darren, when we saw Josh's car drive by. But it wasn't Josh driving."

Detective Reeves leaned forward, suddenly very interested. "Oh? And who was driving, if not Mr. Hawkins?"

The two women exchanged a glance, and Josh felt a chill run down his spine. He had a feeling he knew what was coming.

"Well," Daria said slowly, "that's the strange part. We couldn't really see the driver clearly. But there was someone else in the car. In the backseat."

"Someone we've never seen before," Melanie added. "A man, dressed like he was from another time. Like the '60s or something."

The room fell silent. Josh could feel everyone's eyes on him as the implications of this statement sank in. His own wild story about a ghostly figure suddenly didn't seem so far-fetched.

Detective Reeves cleared his throat. "Ladies, are you saying you saw a... ghost... in Mr. Hawkins's car?"

"We're saying what we saw," Daria replied firmly. "Make of it what you will, Detective. But we know it wasn't Josh driving that car."

Reeves turned to Mike. "And you, Mr. Harris? What's your part in all this?"

Mike straightened in his chair. "I was with Josh the whole time, Detective. We were camping at Lake Shawnee. We just got back when your deputy picked Josh up. He had nothing to do with Darren's death."

The detective was quiet for a long moment, his eyes moving from one face to another, finally settling on Josh. "Well, Mr. Hawkins, it seems you've got quite the support system here. And quite the mystery on our hands."

Josh met the detective's gaze, a mix of relief and apprehension washing over him. "I told you, Detective. I didn't kill Darren. But something strange is going on, and I think... I think it might be connected to my car somehow."

Reeves sighed, rubbing his temples. He handed his business card to Mike. "Alright, folks. I think we've got a lot more to discuss. Mr. Hawkins, consider yourself still under investigation, but for now, you're free to go. Don't leave town. We'll be in touch."

As the group stood to leave, Josh couldn't shake the feeling that this was far from over. The ghost, Darren's death, the mysterious driver – it was all connected somehow. And he had a sinking feeling that he was right in the middle of it all.

Outside the police station, as Mike, Daria, and Melanie gathered around him with concerned faces, Josh made a decision. It was time to get to the bottom of this, once and for all. Whatever was haunting his car, whatever had happened to Darren, he was going to figure it out.

Even if it meant facing the ghostly figure from the '60s himself.

Chapter 10
Piecing the Puzzle

The clock on Josh's living room wall ticked past midnight, its soft rhythm a counterpoint to the chaos of the day's events. Josh sat on his couch, staring blankly at the untouched cup of coffee on the table before him. The house felt unusually quiet, almost oppressive, after the tumult of the police station. A gentle knock at the door startled him from his reverie. Cautiously, he approached, peering through the peephole. His eyebrows raised in surprise as he recognized Daria standing on his porch, hugging herself against the cool night air.

"Daria?" Josh said as he opened the door. "What are you doing here so late?"

She offered a weak smile. "Hey, Josh. I... I couldn't sleep. I keep thinking about what happened, what we saw. Can I come in?"

Josh nodded, stepping aside to let her enter. As she passed, he caught a whiff of her perfume, a subtle floral scent that seemed at odds with the heaviness of the situation.

"Coffee?" he offered, gesturing to the kitchen.

"Please," Daria replied, settling onto the couch.

As Josh busied himself in the kitchen, Daria's eyes roamed the living room, taking in the scattered books on paranormal phenomena and local history that Josh had pulled out earlier in a desperate attempt to make sense of recent events. Returning with two steaming mugs, Josh sat beside her, leaving a respectful distance between them. For a moment, they sipped in silence, the weight of unspoken words hanging in the air.

Finally, Daria spoke. "Josh, I need to tell you something. Something I didn't say at the police station."

Josh tensed, setting his mug down. "What is it?"

Daria took a deep breath. "That night, when Melanie and I saw your car... we didn't just see Darren and that strange man. We... we heard something too."

Josh leaned forward, his heart racing. "What did you hear?"

"It was just for a moment as they passed by," Daria continued, her voice barely above a whisper. "But we heard... laughter. Not normal laughter, Josh. It was... wrong somehow. Cold. And then..." She shuddered. "Then we heard a scream. Darren's scream."

Josh felt a chill run down his spine. "Why didn't you tell the police this?"

Daria shook her head, her eyes glistening with unshed tears. "Would you have believed us? A ghostly figure and phantom sounds? We were scared, Josh. We didn't know what to think."

Josh reached out, hesitantly placing his hand over hers. "I believe you, Daria. Because I've seen him too. The man from the '60s."

Daria's eyes widened. "You have? When?"

"It started a few weeks ago," Josh began, and found himself pouring out the whole story – the first sightings, the growing sense of dread, the tie clip at the campsite. As he spoke, Daria listened intently, occasionally nodding or gasping softly.

When he finished, Daria was quiet for a long moment. Then she asked, "Josh, what did this man look like? The one you saw?"

Josh closed his eyes, trying to recall every detail. "He was young, maybe in his late 20s or early 30s. Always wearing jeans and a t-shirt. Dark hair, slicked back. And his eyes..." Josh shuddered. "His eyes were dark, almost black. But sometimes, when he looked at me, they seemed... empty. Like there was nothing behind them."

Daria's grip on his hand tightened. "That's him. That's exactly who we saw in your car with Darren."

They sat in silence, the implications of this connection sinking in. Finally, Josh spoke, his voice determined. "Daria, we need to figure out who this man is. Or was. There has to be a reason he's haunting my car, a reason he was with Darren that night."

Daria nodded, a spark of determination in her eyes. "Where do we start?"

Josh glanced at the books scattered around the room. "I've been doing some research on local history, trying to find any incidents involving a man matching this description. But maybe we're looking in the wrong place. Maybe..." He trailed off, a thought forming.

"What is it?" Daria prompted.

"The car," Josh said slowly. "We need to look into the history of the car. I bought it second-hand a few years ago, but I don't know much about its previous owners."

Daria straightened up, energized by the idea. "That's a good place to start. We can trace the car's history, see if there were any incidents or deaths associated with it."

As they began to plan their investigation, the atmosphere in the room shifted. The fear and uncertainty were still there, but now there was also a sense of purpose, of forward momentum.

Outside, unnoticed by either of them, a figure stood on the sidewalk, gazing up at Josh's living room window. In the pale moonlight, his 1960s 'Greaser' attire seemed to shimmer, as if not quite solid. A slow, cold smile spread across his face as he watched the two figures inside, planning and theorizing.

The clock ticked steadily towards 2 AM, but neither Josh nor Daria seemed to notice the late hour. They sat close together on the couch, surrounded by books and hastily scribbled notes, the energy of their budding investigation filling the room. As Daria jotted down another potential lead, Josh found himself distracted. The soft glow of the table lamp caught the highlights in her hair, and he was suddenly struck by a memory. He cleared his throat nervously.

"You know," he began, his voice slightly hesitant, "there's something I never told you about the car."

Daria looked up from her notes, curiosity piqued. "Oh? What's that?"

Josh felt a blush creeping up his neck. "Well, the truth is... I kind of bought it to impress you."

Daria's eyebrows shot up in surprise. "Me? Really?"

Josh nodded, a sheepish smile playing at his lips. "Yeah. Remember that day at the campus car show, about three years ago? You were going on about how much you loved classic cars, especially '60s muscle cars. You said your dream car was a '67 Mustang."

Recognition dawned in Daria's eyes. "I remember that day. I can't believe you remembered that conversation."

"Well," Josh continued, his blush deepening, "a few months later, I saw this Mustang for sale. It needed some work, but... I don't know. I thought maybe if I fixed it up, you'd..."

He trailed off, suddenly feeling foolish. But when he looked up, he saw Daria watching him with a soft expression he'd never seen before.

"Josh," she said quietly, "that's incredibly sweet."

Their eyes met, and suddenly the air between them felt charged. Josh became acutely aware of how close they were sitting, of the subtle floral scent of Daria's perfume.

"I've always liked you, Daria," Josh admitted, his voice barely above a whisper. "I just never knew how to tell you."

Daria's hand found his, their fingers intertwining. "I've liked you too, Josh. I just thought... well, with everything that happened with Darren, I wasn't sure if..."

Josh shook his head. "Darren and I were friends, but... it was always you, Daria."

The space between them seemed to shrink. Josh's heart hammered in his chest as Daria leaned in closer. Their lips met in a soft, tentative kiss that quickly deepened, years of unspoken feelings pouring out in a single moment.

When they finally pulled apart, both slightly breathless, Daria rested her forehead against Josh's. "Wow," she murmured.

"Yeah," Josh agreed, a giddy smile spreading across his face.

For a moment, they sat in comfortable silence, reveling in this new development. But reality soon crept back in, and Josh's expression sobered.

"Daria," he said softly, "I want you to know... whatever's going on with this ghost, with Darren's death... I'm going to figure it out. And I'll keep you safe, I promise."

Daria pulled back slightly, her eyes meeting his with a determined gaze. "We'll figure it out together, Josh. I'm not going anywhere."

As if to emphasize her point, she leaned in and kissed him again, this one filled with promise and resolve.

Outside, unseen by the couple, the ghostly figure in the '60s rockabilly attire still stood watching. His dark eyes narrowed at the scene unfolding in the living room, and the temperature around him dropped sharply. Frost began to form on the nearby windows, creeping in intricate patterns across the glass.

The ghost's form flickered, and for a brief moment, his handsome features twisted into something inhuman and terrifying. Then, as quickly as it had appeared, the distortion vanished, leaving only the dapper young man from another time.

The apparition turned away from the house, walking down the empty street with an unnatural grace. As he passed under a streetlight, his form shimmered and vanished, leaving behind only a whisper of cold air and the faint, unsettling echo of distant laughter.

Josh tossed and turned, the sheets tangling around his legs as he fell deeper into an uneasy sleep. In his dream, he found himself standing in a moonlit parking lot, the air thick with an oppressive silence.

A gleaming black Mustang sat motionless in the center of the lot, its chrome accents reflecting the pale light. Josh felt a chill run down his spine as he noticed Daria approaching the vehicle, her movements slow and dreamlike.

"Daria, wait!" he tried to call out, but no sound escaped his lips. He watched in helpless horror as the car's headlights suddenly flared to life, bathing Daria in their harsh glow. The engine roared, a sound more animal than mechanical. As Daria reached for the door handle, the car seemed to shudder and stretch, its form twisting in impossible ways. The chrome trim writhed like serpents, reaching out towards her with malevolent intent.

Josh tried to run towards her, but his feet felt leaden. The distance between them seemed to grow with each step he took. He could only watch as the car's distorted form loomed over Daria, ready to engulf her.

Just as the twisted metal was about to touch her, Josh jolted awake with a strangled cry. His heart pounded in his chest as he sat bolt upright, gasping for air.

"Josh? What's wrong?" Daria's concerned voice cut through the darkness. He felt her hand on his arm, warm and reassuring.

"I... I had a nightmare," he managed to stammer, his voice shaky. "It felt so real."

Daria reached over and switched on the bedside lamp, illuminating the room with a soft glow. Her face was etched with worry as she looked at him. "Do you want to talk about it?"

Josh shook his head, the details of the dream already fading but leaving behind a lingering sense of dread. "No, it's okay. I'm sorry I woke you."

Daria glanced at the clock and sighed. "It's alright. I should be getting up anyway. I have an early shift at work."

As she slipped out of bed and began to gather her things, Josh couldn't shake the uneasy feeling that clung to him. He watched Daria move about the room, remembering how vulnerable she had looked in his dream.

"Be careful today, okay?" he found himself saying as she prepared to leave.

Daria paused at the door, giving him a quizzical look. "Of course. It was just a bad dream.. Try to get some rest."

As the door closed behind her, Josh lay back down, staring at the ceiling. The shadows in the corners of the room seemed deeper than before, and he couldn't help but wonder if the nightmare had been more than just a dream.

Chapter 11

The Phantom Drive

Josh settled into the driver's seat of his Mustang, the familiar leather creaking beneath him. The events of the previous night's nightmare still lingered in his mind, casting a shadow over the sunny afternoon. He needed to talk to someone, to make sense of the growing unease that had taken root in his chest.

With a deep breath, he pulled out his cell phone and dialed Mike's number. The call connected after a few rings.

"Hey, Josh. What's up?" Mike's voice crackled through the speaker.

"Mike, I need to talk. Something weird is going on, and I — " Josh's words caught in his throat as his eyes flicked to the rearview mirror.

There, in the backseat, a translucent figure shimmered into existence. It was a man, dressed in the style of the 1960s – a mix between ragged jeans and a white t-shirt. His hair was slicked back, and a lit cigarette dangled from his fingers, though no smoke rose from it.

But it was his eyes that caught Josh's attention – piercing and intense, fixed on Josh with an unsettling focus.

"Josh? You there, man?" Mike's voice seemed distant now, barely registering in Josh's mind.

The ghostly man's mouth moved, forming words Josh couldn't hear but felt reverberate through his body. His hands began to shake, the phone slipping from his grasp.

"I... I'll call you back," Josh managed to stammer before the phone clattered to the floor.

He blinked hard, hoping the apparition would vanish. When he looked again, the backseat was empty, but the chill remained, seeping into his bones. The faint scent of old tobacco lingered in the air.

Without conscious thought, Josh's hands moved to the ignition. The Mustang roared to life, the engine's rumble deeper and more ominous than he remembered. His foot pressed the accelerator, and the car pulled away from the curb with a sense of purpose that didn't seem to be his own.

As he drove, the streets of Topeka began to blur around him. Josh felt as if he were watching himself from outside his body, unable to control his actions.

The rational part of his mind screamed at him to stop, to turn around, but his hands remained steady on the wheel, guiding the car with unwavering determination.

Buildings gave way to houses, then to open fields as the Mustang ate up the miles. The sun dipped lower on the horizon, painting the sky in shades of crimson and gold. Still, Josh drove on, deeper into the countryside.

The radio crackled to life, cycling through stations of its own accord. Snippets of music filtered through the static – the twang of 60s guitar riffs, the smooth harmonies of doo-wop groups, the raw energy of early rock and roll. It created a disjointed symphony that made Josh's head spin, transporting him to an era he'd never known.

As darkness fell, Josh finally felt the fugue state begin to lift. He blinked, coming back to himself, and realized with a start that he had no idea where he was. Miles of cornfields stretched out on either side of the narrow country road, swaying gently in the evening breeze.

He eased his foot off the accelerator, the Mustang slowing to a stop at the side of the road. With trembling hands, he switched off the ignition. The sudden silence was deafening.

Josh fumbled for his phone, intending to call for help, but found the battery dead. He was alone, lost in the middle of nowhere, with only the stars and the whisper of corn leaves to keep him company.

As he sat there, trying to calm his racing heart, a flicker of movement caught his eye. In the rearview mirror, just for a moment, he thought he saw the ghostly man again. This time, he was smiling, raising an ethereal glass as if in a toast.

Josh squinted, trying to make out more details, but the figure had vanished. All that remained was the faint aroma of aged whiskey and cigarette smoke, a phantom scent from decades past.

Josh blinked rapidly, his senses rushing back as if he'd been doused with ice water. The cornfields on either side of the road were a blur of dark shapes against the night sky. He realized with a start that the Mustang was moving again, accelerating down the narrow country road at an alarming speed.

His hands gripped the steering wheel, knuckles white, but he wasn't the one controlling the car. An unseen force pressed down on the accelerator, the engine roaring as the speedometer climbed.

In the rearview mirror, the ghostly man from the '60s appeared again, his form more solid than before. A malevolent grin spread across his face as he leaned forward, his cold presence enveloping Josh from behind.

"What do you want?" Josh shouted, his voice trembling.

The ghost's only response was a deep, rumbling laugh that seemed to come from the car itself. The temperature in the cabin plummeted, Josh's breath visible in quick, panicked puffs.

Suddenly, an icy grip seized Josh's wrist, trying to wrench his hand from the steering wheel. He fought against it, swerving dangerously close to the edge of the road. The ghost's other hand materialized on Josh's shoulder, the glacial touch burning through his shirt.

The radio blared to life, a cacophony of 1960s rock and roll blasting at full volume. The car's lights flickered erratically, temporarily blinding Josh as he struggled to maintain control.

Through the chaos, Josh caught glimpses of the ghost in his peripheral vision – sometimes in the passenger seat, sometimes in the back, its form shifting and distorting with each appearance. The air grew thick with the overpowering scent of stale cigarettes and whiskey.

In a moment of clarity, Josh saw a turnoff approaching – a dirt road leading into a dense forest. With all his strength, he yanked the steering wheel, sending the

Mustang careening onto the rough path. The ghost's grip faltered as the car bounced and jostled.

Seizing his chance, Josh slammed on the brakes. The Mustang fishtailed, skidding to a stop at the forest's edge. Without a second thought, Josh flung open the door and bolted into the woods.

Branches whipped at his face as he ran, the sound of his pounding heart nearly drowning out the rustling leaves beneath his feet. He dared not look back, fear driving him deeper into the darkness.

After what felt like an eternity, Josh's lungs burned for air, forcing him to slow. He leaned against a large oak tree, gasping for breath. The forest was eerily silent, no sign of pursuit.

As his eyes adjusted to the gloom, Josh realized he was hopelessly lost. The trees loomed around him, their shadows forming grotesque shapes in the faint moonlight. He strained his ears, hoping to hear distant traffic or any sign of civilization, but there was nothing.

A twig snapped somewhere behind him. Josh spun around, peering into the darkness. Was it just an animal, or something more sinister? The ghost's laughter echoed in his memory, sending a shiver down his spine.

Josh knew he couldn't stay put. With no clear direction, he chose a path and started walking, every sense on high alert. Each shadow held a potential threat, every rustle of leaves a possible sign of the supernatural force that seemed determined to claim him.

As he pushed through the underbrush, one thought repeated in Josh's mind: What was the connection between this ghost, the Mustang, and himself? The answer, he feared, lay somewhere in this forest – or back with the car he'd left behind.

Mike paced his living room, phone pressed to his ear as he listened to the endless ringing. This was his third attempt to reach Josh in the last hour, each call going straight to voicemail.

The abrupt end to their earlier conversation replayed in his mind, Josh's panicked tone setting off alarm bells.

With a frustrated sigh, he ended the call and scrolled through his contacts. His thumb hovered over Daria's name for a moment before he hit dial.

Daria answered on the second ring. "Mike? Is everything okay?"

"Hey, Daria. I'm worried about Josh," Mike said, cutting straight to the chase. "I was on the phone with him earlier, and he suddenly hung up. Sounded scared. Now I can't reach him at all."

There was a pause on the other end of the line. When Daria spoke again, her voice was tight with concern.

"When did you last talk to him? Did he say anything strange?"

Mike frowned, trying to recall the details. "It was a few hours ago. He said he needed to talk, that something weird was going on. But before he could explain, he just... stopped. Then he said he'd call back and hung up."

"Oh no," Daria whispered. "Mike, there's something you need to know. Josh has been acting strange lately. He's been having nightmares, and..." She hesitated, as if unsure whether to continue.

"And what?" Mike prompted.

"He mentioned seeing a ghost," Daria said quickly. "In the Mustang. I thought it was just stress from Darren's death, but now I'm not so sure."

Mike felt a chill run down his spine. "Wait, Josh told me about a ghost too. I thought he was just messing around, but he seemed pretty shaken up about it."

"He told you?" Daria's voice rose in pitch. "When?"

"A couple of days ago. He said he saw some guy from the '60s in the backseat. I told him he was probably just tired, seeing things."

The line went quiet for a moment. When Daria spoke again, her voice was resolute. "Mike, this can't be a coincidence. First Darren's accident, then these ghost sightings, and now Josh is unreachable. Something is very wrong."

Mike nodded, even though Daria couldn't see him. "I agree. But what can we do? It's not like we can file a missing persons report yet."

"Maybe not," Daria said slowly, "but we can talk to the police. Tell them about our concerns, about the strange things that have been happening. Even if they can't do anything officially, they might be able to help us figure out where to start looking for Josh."

Mike considered this. It wasn't much of a plan, but it was better than sitting around doing nothing. "Alright, let's do it. Can you meet me at the police station in 30 minutes?"

"I'll be there," Daria confirmed. "And Mike? Bring anything you have that might help – phone records, text messages, anything that shows Josh's state of mind recently."

"Got it. See you soon."

As Mike ended the call, he felt a mix of relief and apprehension. Relief that he and Daria were taking action, but apprehension about what they might uncover. He gathered his phone, laptop, and a notebook filled with recent conversations with Josh.

Before heading out, Mike paused at his front door. His eyes fell on an old photo of him and Josh standing proudly next to the Mustang the day Josh bought it.

"Hang in there, buddy," Mike murmured. "We're coming for you."

Chapter 12
The Chase

The forest seemed to close in around Josh as he stumbled through the undergrowth. Branches clawed at his clothes, roots threatened to trip him with every step. His lungs burned, and his legs ached, but fear drove him onward. The memory of the ghost's icy touch spurred him to keep moving, even as exhaustion threatened to overwhelm him.

A faint rustling behind him sent a jolt of adrenaline through his body. Was it the wind, or something more sinister? Josh didn't dare look back to find out. He pushed forward, his feet pounding against the forest floor.

In his haste, he failed to notice a gnarled root protruding from the earth. His foot caught, and suddenly the world tilted. Josh tumbled forward, landing hard on the damp ground. Pain shot through his palms as they scraped against rough stones and twigs.

Gasping for breath, Josh rolled onto his back, expecting at any moment to feel the ghost's glacial presence. But as he looked up, his eyes widened in surprise.

There, barely ten feet away, stood the spectral figure of the 1960s man. But something was different. The ghost wasn't advancing. Instead, it seemed to be straining against an invisible barrier, its form flickering and distorting as if it were a bad television signal.

Josh scrambled backward, putting more distance between himself and the apparition. As he did, he noticed the ghost's eyes weren't fixed on him. Instead, the specter was gazing intently at something in the distance, beyond the line it couldn't seem to cross.

Following the ghost's line of sight, Josh felt a jolt of recognition. Through a break in the trees, he could make out the silhouette of a familiar place: Old Willie's Auto Salvage, the very junkyard where he had purchased the Mustang months ago.

"What is it?" Josh found himself asking, his voice hoarse. "What are you trying to show me?"

The ghost's head snapped toward him, its piercing eyes locking onto Josh's for a moment. There was an intensity in that gaze, a mixture of frustration and urgency that sent a shiver down Josh's spine. The specter's mouth moved, but no sound came out.

"I don't understand," Josh said, slowly getting to his feet. "Is there something at the junkyard? Something to do with the Mustang?"

At the mention of the car, the ghost's form seemed to solidify slightly. It made a gesture as if to speak again, but then abruptly turned away. With one last, long look toward the junkyard, the spectral figure began to walk back in the direction they had come from, toward where the Mustang was parked.

Josh watched, bewildered, as the ghost faded into the darkness of the forest. The oppressive atmosphere that had accompanied the specter's presence lifted, leaving behind an eerie calm.

For a long moment, Josh stood rooted to the spot, his mind racing. The ghost's behavior, its apparent inability to cross some invisible line, and its fixation on the junkyard – it all had to mean something. But what?

As the adrenaline began to wear off, Josh became acutely aware of his surroundings. He was alone in the forest, in the middle of the night, with no clear way back to civilization. But now, at least, he had a landmark to orient himself.

With a deep breath, Josh turned toward the distant silhouette of Old Willie's Auto Salvage. Whatever answers he was looking for, they seemed to lie in that direction. As he took his first tentative steps toward the junkyard, a mixture of fear and determination settled in his gut. He was walking into the unknown, but it was his only path forward.

Josh's feet crunched on fallen leaves as he made his way back through the forest. The junkyard's silhouette had disappeared behind him, obscured by the dense foliage. His mind raced, trying to piece together the puzzle of the ghost, the Mustang, and Old Willie's Auto Salvage.

As he pushed through a thicket, a familiar glint caught his eye - moonlight reflecting off chrome. The Mustang sat where he had left it, a dark silhouette against the night sky. Josh felt a mixture of relief and apprehension as he approached his car.

"Just get in and drive away," he muttered to himself, trying to summon courage. "Figure everything else out later."

He was barely ten yards from the Mustang when the temperature plummeted. His breath misted in front of him, and an all-too-familiar chill ran down his spine. Before he could react, the spectral figure materialized between him and the car.

The ghost's appearance had changed. Gone was the confused, almost lost expression from earlier. Now, its face was contorted in anger, eyes blazing with an otherworldly light. It raised an arm, pointing at Josh in an unmistakable gesture: Stay away.

"What do you want?" Josh called out, his voice shaking. "Why won't you let me near my car?"

The ghost's mouth moved, but instead of words, a bone-chilling howl filled the air. The sound was full of rage and desperation, causing Josh to stumble backward in fear.

As if spurred by Josh's retreat, the ghost surged forward. Its form seemed more solid now, more threatening. It moved with purpose, driving Josh back towards the forest.

Josh's survival instincts kicked in. He turned and ran, branches whipping at his face as he plunged back into the woods. Behind him, he could hear the ghost's pursuit - a sound like rushing wind mixed with that awful, angry howl.

As he ran, Josh's mind whirled. The ghost's behavior had changed dramatically. In the forest, it had seemed unable to approach him, even appeared to be trying to communicate. But now, near the Mustang, it had become aggressive, almost protective of the car.

"It doesn't want me near the Mustang," Josh gasped between breaths. The realization hit him hard. Whatever connection existed between the ghost and the car, it was clear the spirit considered the Mustang off-limits to Josh.

He ran until his lungs burned and his legs trembled with exhaustion. Finally, he allowed himself to slow, listening intently for any sign of pursuit. The forest had grown quiet again, the ghost's howls fading into the night.

Josh leaned against a tree, gulping in air. He was lost, separated from his car, and no closer to understanding the supernatural events plaguing him. But one thing was clear - the Mustang was at the center of it all.

As his breathing steadied, Josh looked around, trying to get his bearings. In the distance, through a gap in the trees, he thought he could make out lights. Civilization, or at least a road. It wasn't much, but it was a start.

With one last glance over his shoulder, Josh set off toward the lights. The ghost seemed determined to keep him away from the Mustang, but there had to be answers somewhere. Maybe at Old Willie's Auto Salvage, or perhaps with Daria and Mike.

As he walked, a grim determination settled over Josh. He would find a way to break this haunting, to reclaim his car and his life. But first, he had to survive the night and find his way back to town.

The first hints of dawn were starting to lighten the sky as Josh trudged along the side of the road. His clothes were damp with dew, and leaves clung to his jacket - silent witnesses to his night in the forest.

Every few minutes, he'd pull out his phone, hoping to see bars of reception appear, but the screen remained stubbornly empty.

"Some 5G network," Josh muttered, shoving the useless device back into his pocket. He'd been walking for what felt like hours, but the road seemed endless, stretching into the distance with no signs of town in sight.

The rumble of an engine broke the morning silence. Josh turned, hope rising in his chest at the sight of headlights approaching. As the vehicle drew closer, he recognized the distinctive shape of a tow truck. Its metal frame glinted in the early light, the name "Willie's Auto Salvage" barely visible on its side.

The truck slowed as it approached, and Josh got a good look at the driver. Behind the wheel sat an old man, his weathered face framed by a scraggly white beard. A worn baseball cap sat atop his head, and his eyes twinkled with curiosity as he pulled up alongside Josh.

"Well, ain't you a sight for sore eyes," the old man called out, his voice gravelly but warm. "What are you doing out here at this hour?"

Josh hesitated for a moment, unsure how much to reveal. "I, uh... had some car trouble," he said finally. It wasn't entirely a lie.

The old man chuckled. "Car trouble, eh? Well, you're in luck. How about I give you a lift? We can take a look at your car if you'd like."

Josh's heart skipped a beat at the mention of Old Willie's. This was the very junkyard where he'd bought the Mustang, the place the ghost had seemed so fixated on. Could this be a coincidence?

"That's... that's very kind of you," Josh said, trying to keep his voice steady.

Old Willie's eyebrows shot up. "The '67 Ford? I remember that beauty. Shame to see her go, but glad she found a good home." He patted the passenger seat. "Hop in, son. Seems like we've got some catching up to do."

Josh hesitated for a split second, weighing his options. On one hand, getting into a stranger's vehicle seemed risky. On the other, Old Willie might have information about the Mustang's history - information that could help explain the haunting.

Making his decision, Josh climbed into the truck. The cab smelled of old leather and motor oil, a scent that was oddly comforting after the long night in the woods.

As Willie put the truck in gear and they started moving, he glanced sideways at Josh. "So, tell me about this 'car trouble' of yours. That Mustang giving you grief?"

Josh took a deep breath. How much should he reveal? The truth would sound crazy, but something told him that Old Willie might be more understanding than most.

"It's... complicated," Josh began. "You're going to think I'm nuts, but... have you ever heard of a car being haunted?"

To Josh's surprise, Old Willie didn't laugh or scoff. Instead, the old man's face grew serious, his grip tightening slightly on the steering wheel.

"Son," Willie said slowly, "in my line of work, you hear all sorts of stories. Some crazier than others." He paused, seeming to choose his next words carefully. "That Mustang... she's got quite a history. More than you might think."

As the tow truck rumbled down the road towards Old Willie's Auto Salvage, Josh felt a mixture of anticipation and dread. Whatever secrets the Mustang held, he sensed he was about to uncover them.

Josh started to rethink about some of the recent events that led him to this moment. Was he becoming a failure? Was he cursed with bad luck? He wondered if other people had to deal with the amount of absurd and random negative things all collide at once. How would anyone else react to all of this, let alone survive emotionally? Josh just hoped he was ready for the truth.

Chapter 13
A Chilling Discovery

The full moon cast an eerie glow over the deserted country road as Melanie's sedan cruised through the night. She was on her way home from a late shift at the diner, her mind already drifting to the comfort of her bed, when something caught her eye.

A sleek black shape sat just off the road, partially hidden by the shadows of overhanging trees. Melanie slowed down, squinting through her windshield. As she passed, recognition dawned – it was Josh's Mustang.

"What the hell?" she muttered, pulling over to the shoulder. She knew Josh; they'd gone to high school together. What was his car doing out here in the middle of nowhere at this hour?

Melanie made a U-turn, her headlights sweeping across the empty road. As she approached the Mustang again, she felt a growing sense of unease. The car sat silent and dark, with no sign of Josh or anyone else nearby.

She pulled up behind the Mustang and cut her engine. The sudden silence was oppressive, broken only by the soft ticking of her cooling engine and the rustling of leaves in the light breeze.

"Josh?" Melanie called out as she stepped from her car. No response.

She approached the Mustang cautiously, her phone's flashlight cutting through the darkness. The car seemed undamaged, just parked at an odd angle as if its driver had pulled over in a hurry.

As Melanie reached for the driver's side door handle, the temperature around her plummeted. Her breath clouded in front of her face, and she shivered violently, the sudden cold piercing through her thin waitress uniform.

A movement in her peripheral vision made her whirl around. For a split second, she thought she saw a figure standing at the edge of the woods – a man in old-fashioned clothes, his form somehow blurred and indistinct in the moonlight.

"Hello?" Melanie's voice quavered. "Is someone there?"

The figure didn't respond. Instead, it seemed to flicker like a faulty lightbulb before disappearing entirely.

126

Melanie's heart raced. She backed away from the Mustang, her eyes darting between the car and the spot where she'd seen the figure. The woods seemed to loom closer, shadows twisting into menacing shapes.

A twig snapped in the forest, the sound unnaturally loud in the still night air. Melanie jumped, dropping her phone. As she bent to retrieve it, she noticed something that made her blood run cold – a set of footprints in the soft earth leading from the Mustang into the woods. But they weren't normal footprints. They seemed to fade in and out, as if the person who made them was only partially there.

That was enough for Melanie. She scrambled back to her car, hands shaking as she fumbled with her keys. As she slammed the door shut, she could have sworn she heard a low, mournful whisper carried on the wind.

Melanie's tires squealed as she pulled away, her mind reeling. She needed to tell someone what she'd seen. But who would believe her?

In her rearview mirror, the Mustang faded into the distance, a dark silhouette against the moonlit night. For a moment, Melanie thought she saw the figure again, standing next to the car. But when she blinked, it was gone.

The interior of Willie's office was a cluttered testament to decades in the auto salvage business. Stacks of yellowed invoices teetered on a battered desk, while the walls were adorned with vintage car parts and faded photographs. The air was thick with the scent of old paper and motor oil.

Josh settled into a creaky chair across from Willie, his eyes darting around the room, taking in every detail. His gaze lingered on a wall covered in photographs – snapshots of cars and their proud owners, each telling a story of its own.

Willie lowered himself into his chair with a grunt. "So, you wanted to know about that Mustang of yours, eh? She's got quite a tale to tell."

Josh leaned forward, his fatigue momentarily forgotten. "Yes, please. Anything you can tell me would be helpful."

Willie's eyes took on a distant look, as if peering into the past. "That car came to us back in '88. Belonged to a young fella named Clint Perkins. He was quite the character – local racing champion, bit of a daredevil."

As Willie spoke, Josh's eyes were drawn to a particular photograph on the wall. It showed a young man leaning against the Mustang, a trophy in his hand and a cocky grin on his face. The image was slightly faded, but there was no mistaking the resemblance to the ghostly figure that had been haunting Josh.

Willie continued, oblivious to Josh's growing unease. "Clint loved that car more than anything. Spent every spare minute tuning her up, making her faster. But you know how it is with daredevils – always pushing the limits."

Josh swallowed hard. "What happened to him?"

Willie's face grew somber. "It was a freak accident. Clint was working on the car late one night – always did prefer to tinker after hours. Something went wrong. By the time I got here the next morning..." He trailed off, shaking his head.

"Was he...?" Josh couldn't bring himself to finish the question.

"Dead as a doornail," Willie confirmed. "Looked like the jack had failed while he was underneath. Crushed him. It was a shame. That boy had his whole life ahead of him."

Josh felt a chill run down his spine. The pieces were starting to fall into place – the ghost's appearance, its attachment to the car, its aggressive behavior when Josh tried to approach the Mustang.

Willie seemed lost in thought for a moment, then chuckled softly. "You know, it's the strangest thing. After Clint died, I could never bring myself to sell that car. It sat in the yard for years. Folks would come looking to buy, but something always fell through. It was like the car was waiting for the right person."

He fixed Josh with a penetrating gaze. "Then you came along. The moment you laid eyes on that Mustang, I knew she was meant for you. Funny how things work out, isn't it?"

Josh forced a weak smile, his mind reeling. "Yeah, funny," he managed. The room suddenly felt too small, too confining. He needed air. "Um, would you mind if I stepped outside for a moment? Just need some fresh air after the long night."

Willie nodded, concern creasing his weathered face. "Of course, son. Take all the time you need. We can talk more when you're ready."

Josh rose on shaky legs and made his way to the door. As he stepped outside, the cool morning air hit his face, but it did little to calm the turmoil in his mind.

He leaned against the wall of the office, his eyes scanning the junkyard. Somewhere out there was his Mustang – and possibly the restless spirit of Clint Perkins. Josh took a deep breath, trying to steady himself.

He now knew the source of the haunting, but this revelation brought more questions than answers. Why was Clint's spirit bound to the car? And more importantly, how could Josh put him to rest and reclaim his life?

The fluorescent lights of the police station buzzed overhead as Mike and Daria sat across from Detective Ferguson. The detective's office was small but tidy, with filing cabinets lining one wall and a cork board covered in notes and photos on another.

Detective Ferguson, a woman in her mid-forties with sharp eyes and graying hair pulled back in a tight bun, leaned forward on her desk. "So, let me get this straight," she said, her tone a mixture of skepticism and curiosity. "Your friend Josh has gone missing, and you believe it's connected to... a ghost?"

Mike and Daria exchanged glances. Mike turned back to Detective Ferguson. "What happened to Detective Reeves? We were talking to him before."

"Retired," Ferguson responded sharply. "So, this ghost?"

"We know how it sounds," Mike began, "but there's something really strange going on. Josh has been acting weird ever since he bought that old Mustang."

Daria nodded. "He's been having nightmares, seeing things. And now we can't reach him."

Detective Ferguson raised an eyebrow. "Seeing things? Can you elaborate on that?"

Daria took a deep breath. "Josh said he saw a ghost in his car. A man, dressed like he was from the 1960s. Young, maybe in his twenties."

At this, Detective Ferguson' expression changed subtly. She leaned back in her chair, studying Daria intently. "This ghost... did Josh describe him in any more detail?"

Daria closed her eyes, trying to recall Josh's words. "He said the man had slicked-back dark hair, kind of a James Dean look. Wearing a white T-shirt and jeans. Josh mentioned he looked... angry, or frustrated."

Detective Ferguson was silent for a moment, her fingers drumming on the desk. Then, without a word, she turned to one of the filing cabinets behind her. Mike and Daria watched as she rifled through a drawer, finally pulling out a manila folder.

"I want you to look at something," Detective Ferguson said, her voice carefully neutral. She opened the folder and slid a photograph across the desk.

Daria leaned forward to look, and her eyes widened in shock. The photo showed a young man leaning against a classic car, his hair slicked back, wearing a white T-shirt and jeans. His face bore a cocky grin, but there was an intensity in his eyes that was almost unsettling.

"That's... that's him," Daria gasped. "That's the man Josh described. But how...?"

Detective Ferguson sat back, her face grave. "This is Clint Perkins. He was a local racing champion back in the '80s. Died in an accident at an auto salvage yard in 1988."

Mike leaned in to look at the photo. "Wait, I recognize that car. That's Josh's Mustang, isn't it?"

Detective Ferguson nodded. "The very same. Clint was the original owner."

"But why do you have his photo in your files?" Daria asked, her voice shaky. "And how did you know to look for it?"

The detective was quiet for a moment, seeming to weigh her words carefully. "Let's just say... yours isn't the first ghost story I've heard about Clint Perkins and that Mustang. Over the years, there have been... incidents. Nothing concrete, nothing we could ever officially act on. But enough to keep a file."

Mike and Daria sat in stunned silence, trying to process this information.

"So you believe us?" Mike finally asked.

Detective Ferguson sighed. "I believe that something is going on, something that's putting your friend in danger. And I think it's time we got to the bottom of it." She stood up, closing the file. "I think we need to pay a visit to Willie's Auto Salvage. That's where Clint died, and where Josh bought the car. If there are answers to be found, they'll be there."

As they prepared to leave, Daria couldn't shake the image of Clint's face from her mind. The cocky young man in the photo seemed a far cry from the angry spirit

Josh had described. What had happened to change him?

And most importantly, what did he want with Josh?

Chapter 14
Ghosts in the Junkyard

Josh's boots crunched on gravel as he wandered through Willie's Junkyard. The setting sun cast long shadows across piles of rusted metal and discarded machinery, transforming the landscape into a maze of grotesque silhouettes.

An eerie stillness hung in the air, broken only by the occasional creak of settling metal or the distant caw of a crow.

Josh had come here seeking answers about the ghostly apparition that had been haunting his prized '67 Ford Mustang. For weeks now, he'd catch glimpses of a spectral face in the rearview mirror, hear whispers emanating from the radio even when it was turned off.

The local mechanics had found nothing wrong with the car, and Josh was at his wit's end.

Willie, the junkyard's owner, had been cryptic when Josh called earlier. "Come by at sunset," he'd growled. "Might have some answers for ya." But now, as Josh picked his way through the automotive graveyard, Willie was nowhere to be seen.

As he rounded a corner, Josh froze. Before him stood a solitary headstone, jarringly out of place among the mechanical debris. Moss clung to its edges, and weeds sprouted from cracks in its base. Approaching cautiously, he read the name etched in weathered stone: Clint Perkins.

His breath caught in his throat as his eyes fell on the faded photograph embedded in the granite. The face staring back at him was hauntingly familiar - the same ghostly visage that had been appearing in his Mustang. Sharp cheekbones, hollow eyes, and a thin-lipped smile that seemed to hold secrets.

A chill ran down Josh's spine as the pieces clicked into place. Clint must be related to Willie somehow. But why was he buried here, in the junkyard? And what connection did he have to Josh's car?

Lost in thought, Josh didn't hear the approaching footsteps behind him. The hairs on the back of his neck stood up, a primal warning coming a moment too late.

Suddenly, a sharp pain exploded at the base of his skull. Stars burst across his vision as he stumbled forward, his hands scraping against the rough surface of the headstone as he tried to catch himself.

As darkness began to engulf him, Josh managed to turn his head. Through rapidly blurring vision, he caught a glimpse of Willie's face, usually impassive, now twisted in a sinister grin. The old man's eyes glinted with a malevolence Josh had never seen before.

"Sorry, boy," Willie's gravelly voice seemed to come from far away. "Can't have you pokin' around where you don't belong. Clint's got plans for that car of yours, and for you."

Josh tried to speak, to ask what Willie meant, but his tongue felt thick and unresponsive. The world tilted sideways as he collapsed to the ground. The last thing he saw before consciousness fled was the photograph on the headstone.

In the deepening twilight, Josh could have sworn Clint's eyes moved, focusing on him with hungry anticipation.

Darkness claimed him then, but it wasn't the peaceful blackness of unconsciousness. Josh felt as if he were falling through an endless void, spectral whispers echoing around him.

Somewhere in the distance, he heard the rumble of a familiar engine – his Mustang. But there was something wrong with the sound, a hellish screech underlying the purr he knew so well.

As Josh tumbled through the abyss of unconsciousness, one thought burned in his fading mind: he was no longer just fighting to understand the haunting of his car.

Consciousness returned to Josh like a sluggish tide, bringing with it a throbbing pain at the base of his skull. He groaned, his eyes fluttering open to a world that refused to come into focus. The acrid smell of motor oil and rusted metal filled his nostrils, mingling with the mustiness of old papers and dust.

As his vision cleared, Josh realized he was lying on a torn leather couch in what appeared to be an office. Dim light filtered through grimy windows, illuminating filing cabinets and shelves cluttered with automotive manuals and spare parts. The junkyard office, he surmised, his mind still foggy.

"Josh? Oh, thank God you're awake!"

A familiar voice cut through his disorientation. Melanie's face swam into view, her brow furrowed with concern. She knelt beside the couch, pressing a cool cloth to his forehead.

"Mel?" Josh croaked, his throat dry. "What are you doing here? How did you find me?"

"Shh, it's okay," Melanie soothed, her hand gentle on his arm. "I got worried when you didn't answer my calls. I remembered you mentioned coming to the junkyard, so I drove out here. Found you passed out by that... that gravestone."

The events before his blackout came rushing back. The headstone. Clint's photograph. Willie's attack.

"Mel, we've got to get out of here," Josh said urgently, trying to sit up despite the wave of dizziness that washed over him. "It's not safe. Old Willie, he's involved in something... something bad. And there's a ghost, Clint—he's been haunting my car, and —"

"Whoa, slow down," Melanie interrupted, placing a hand on his chest to keep him from rising. "You're not making any sense, Josh. You must have hit your head pretty hard when you fell. There's no ghost, and Willie's just a harmless old man."

Josh shook his head vehemently, instantly regretting the motion as pain lanced through his skull. "No, you don't understand. I saw it, Mel. The headstone, Clint's picture – it's the same face I've been seeing in my car. And Willie, he attacked me. We need to leave, now!"

Something shifted in Melanie's expression then, a flicker of... was that amusement? The hand on his chest, once comforting, now felt like a restraint.

"Oh, Josh," Melanie sighed, her voice taking on a patronizing tone that sent a chill down his spine. "I was hoping we could do this the easy way. But you just had to go digging, didn't you?"

"Mel, what—" Josh began, confusion and fear mingling in his gut.

Melanie stood abruptly, moving towards the office door. "Grandpa!" she called out, her voice echoing through the junkyard beyond. "He's awake. Looks like we're doing this the hard way after all."

Josh's blood ran cold as he heard heavy footsteps approaching. He struggled to get up from the couch, his limbs feeling like lead.

"Why, Melanie?" he managed to gasp out. "What's going on?"

Melanie turned back to him, a cruel smile playing on her lips. "Let's just say Clint's got plans, Josh. Big plans. And that car of yours? It's the key to everything."

The office door creaked open, revealing Willie's hulking form. The old man's eyes glinted with the same malevolence Josh had seen before losing consciousness.

"Time for a little trip to the car compactor, boy," Willie growled, advancing into the room.

Josh's struggles were futile against Willie's iron grip. The old man's strength belied his age as he dragged Josh out of the office and into the deepening twilight of the junkyard. Melanie followed close behind, her face a mask of cold determination.

"Where are you taking me?" Josh gasped, his feet scraping against the gravel.

"Shut it, boy," Willie growled, yanking Josh forward. "You'll find out soon enough."

As they weaved through towering piles of junked cars, a massive shape loomed ahead. Josh's heart sank as he recognized the hulking form of an industrial car compactor, its metal jaws gaping open like some monstrous beast.

"Please," Josh pleaded, his voice cracking. "Why are you doing this?"

Melanie stepped forward, her eyes gleaming with a mixture of excitement and what might have been regret. "I suppose you deserve to know the truth, Josh. After all, you've become an unwitting part of our little... project."

She paced alongside them as Willie continued to drag Josh towards the compactor. "That ghost you kept seeing? That was Clint, my mother's old boyfriend. He was obsessed with the 1960s, especially the rockabilly culture. Always dressing like those 'greasers' from back then, with his slicked-back hair and leather jacket."

Josh's mind raced, connecting the dots. The spectral figure in his rearview mirror, the haunting presence in his '67 Mustang – it all started to make a twisted kind of sense.

Melanie continued, her voice taking on a wistful tone. "Clint was... intense. Possessive. He couldn't stand the thought of me being with anyone else. One night, things got out of hand. Grandpa Willie," she gestured to the old man, "he stepped in to protect me. Things went too far, and, well..." She trailed off, leaving the grim conclusion unspoken.

Willie stepped in, continuing the story. "That young punk Cliff took my daughter away, and ended up killing her! They drove into a tree..." Willie started to build tears in his eyes. "We took good care of my daughter. But Cliff, well he got a burial befitting of him."

Willie grunted, his grip on Josh tightening. "Buried him here in the far side of the junkyard. Thought that'd be the end of it."

"But it wasn't, was it?" Josh said, his voice barely above a whisper.

Melanie shook her head. "No, it wasn't. Clint started appearing as a ghost, haunting me. At first, just glimpses, but it got worse. He was angry, vengeful. We tried everything to get rid of him, but nothing worked. Until..."

They reached the car compactor. Willie roughly shoved Josh against its metal frame, the cold steel pressing against his back.

"Until what?" Josh asked, dreading the answer.

Melanie's eyes gleamed with a fervent light. "Until we discovered that Clint's spirit was drawn to certain objects from his era. Especially cars. Your Mustang, Josh – it's perfect. The exact model and year Clint always dreamed of owning. We've been... experimenting. Selling the car off, seeing what happens."

Josh felt a chill that had nothing to do with the cool night air. "You've been letting people die with this ghost in a car? Why?"

Willie sighed, a harsh, grating sound. "You have any idea what a spirit can do to drive others mad? The things we had to endure?"

"But we needed a stronger binding," Melanie added, her voice dropping to a near whisper. "Something to tie Clint's spirit permanently to get him away from us forever. Something like... a fresh soul."

The implications hit Josh like a physical blow. He renewed his struggles against Willie's grip, panic giving him strength. "You're insane! Both of you!"

Willie backhanded Josh, sending him reeling. As Josh's vision swam, he saw Melanie approach, something glinting in her hand – an old key, its metal corroded and discolored.

"This was Clint's," she explained, almost tenderly. "The key to his first car. With this, your blood, and the power of the compactor... we'll bind Clint to your Mustang forever. Don't worry, Josh. Your death will serve a greater purpose."

As Willie began to place Josh inside the compactor's waiting jaws, Josh knew he was out of time. Once again, he found himself praying. However, this time he began to think about miracles, and how this would be a great time for one to come his way.

Josh realized that the simple fact that he was praying for miracles was a clear indication that he was out of options.

Chapter 15
The Crossroads of Fate

The junkyard air crackled with tension as Melanie's shrill voice cut through the night. "Turn it on, Grandpa! Do it now!" Her face, once beautiful, was contorted with a manic desperation that made Josh's blood run cold.

Willie's massive hand hovered over the compactor's control panel, trembling slightly. His weathered face was a battlefield of emotions – fear, doubt, and a flicker of something that might have been remorse.

"I... I don't know, Mel," Willie's gravelly voice was uncharacteristically hesitant. "This ain't right. We've gone too far."

Melanie's eyes flashed dangerously. "Too far? We passed 'too far' years ago, old man. We can't stop now."

Josh, still pinned against the compactor's cold metal frame, saw an opening. He locked eyes with Willie, searching for any hint of humanity in the old man's gaze.

"Willie, please," Josh pleaded, his voice hoarse. "You don't have to do this. Whatever hold Melanie has on you, whatever happened in the past – it's not worth another murder. You can still walk away."

Willie's resolve seemed to waver. His hand dropped from the control panel, and he took a halting step back.

Melanie let out a feral scream. "You weak old fool! After everything we've been through, you're going to let this boy ruin it all?" She lunged for the control panel herself.

In that chaotic moment, as Melanie's fingers reached for the switches that would seal Josh's fate, the air around them suddenly dropped to a bone-chilling cold. A low, unearthly moan echoed through the junkyard, causing all three of them to freeze in place.

The shadows between the piles of junked cars began to writhe and coalesce. A figure stepped forth – a man, or what had once been a man. He was dressed in the classic "greaser" style of the 1960s – leather jacket, slicked-back hair, and a menacing sneer. But his form flickered and wavered like a bad television signal, and his eyes burned with an otherworldly light.

Clint had arrived.

146

Melanie's face drained of all color. "Clint," she whispered, a mixture of fear and longing in her voice.

The ghost's gaze swept over the scene – Willie's guilty stance, Melanie's outstretched hand on the compactor controls, and Josh's terrified form trapped against the machine. When Clint spoke, his voice echoed as if coming from the bottom of a deep, dark well.

"Well, well," the spectral greaser drawled, a bitter smile twisting his translucent features. "Looks like I'm just in time for the party. Did you miss me, baby?"

As Clint's form solidified, the air around them grew heavier, charged with supernatural energy. Josh realized with a sinking feeling that the confrontation he'd been dreading was just beginning. The ghost's arrival hadn't saved him – it had raised the stakes of this deadly game.

Willie backed away, his eyes wide with terror. Melanie stood transfixed, torn between fear and a perverse kind of joy. Josh, still trapped and helpless, knew that his fate now rested in the hands of a vengeful spirit.

The junkyard now stood at the crossroads of the living and the dead. As Clint's ghostly laughter echoed through the night, Josh braced himself for whatever nightmarish turn this encounter would take next.

The tense standoff stretched on, the air thick with supernatural energy and unspoken accusations. Suddenly, Willie's trembling hand left the compactor controls, pointing towards the spectral figure.

"M-Melanie," he stammered, his gruff voice quavering. "Look! It's really him. Clint's here!"

Melanie whirled around, her eyes wide with a mixture of fear, longing, and something darker. She took a halting step towards the ghostly greaser, her composure crumbling with each movement.

"Clint," she whispered, tears welling up in her eyes. "Oh God, Clint. I... I never wanted it to be like this. But you killed my mother!"

Clint's ethereal laughter cut through the air once more, sending chills down Josh's spine. The ghost's form flickered, his edges blurring like a mirage in the heat.

"Didn't want it to be like what?" Clint's voice dripped with bitter sarcasm. "Didn't want to kill me? Or didn't want me to find out about your little... projects?"

Melanie fell to her knees, sobs wracking her body. "You don't understand! I had to do it, Clint. What happened all those years ago... you left me no choice!"

Josh and Willie watched in silence as Melanie's carefully constructed facade shattered completely. "You were out of control, Clint! Your anger, that rage...

I couldn't take it anymore. That night, when you threatened to kill us both...and you went and killed my mother!"

Her confession hung in the air, heavy and damning. Willie's face contorted in shock and betrayal.

"You... you told me he attacked you," the old man growled.

Melanie's tear-streaked face turned to Willie, desperation clear in her eyes. "I'm sorry, Willie. I needed your help. I couldn't... I couldn't face it alone."

All the while, Clint's laughter grew louder, more maniacal. The sound seemed to come from everywhere at once, filling the junkyard with its eerie resonance. Melanie clutched at her head, her eyes wild.

"Stop it!" she screamed. "Why won't you just stay dead?!"

Clint's form solidified once more, his spectral eyes burning with an otherworldly fire. "Oh, I'm dead alright. But I'm not going anywhere. Not until everyone knows what you did."

Clint raised his translucent arm, pointing behind him. In the distance, barely visible beyond the piles of junked cars, flashing lights cut through the darkness. The wail of sirens, faint but growing louder, reached their ears.

"Looks like we've got company," Clint sneered. "Better get your story straight, Mel. The boys in blue are mighty interested in cold cases these days."

Panic erupted in the small group. Willie stumbled backwards, his eyes darting between Melanie and the approaching police lights. Melanie scrambled to her feet, her face a mask of terror and desperation.

Josh, seeing his opportunity in the chaos, wrenched himself free from his position against the compactor. He stumbled away from the machine, putting distance between himself and the others.

The police sirens grew louder. Willie, rooted to the spot in shock; Josh, poised on the edge of death; and Clint's ghost, watching it all unfold with grim satisfaction.

As the police sirens grew louder, panic overtook Melanie. Her eyes, wild with desperation, locked onto the compactor's control panel. She lunged towards it, her fingers stretched for the button that would seal Josh's fate.

"No more loose ends!" she screamed.

Willie, snapping out of his shock, moved with surprising speed for his age. He grabbed Melanie's arm, yanking her away from the controls. "That's enough!" he roared, his face a mask of anger and betrayal. "No more killin'!"

Melanie fought against his grip like a cornered animal, clawing and thrashing. In the struggle, Willie shoved her hard, sending her stumbling backwards. She crashed into a rusted metal stand off to the side of the compactor, the impact echoing through the junkyard.

Taking advantage of the chaos, Josh, who had been slowly working at his bonds, finally managed to free himself. With trembling limbs, he scrambled out of the compactor, putting distance between himself and the machine that had nearly become his tomb.

A terrible groaning sound cut through the night air, drowning out even the approaching sirens. Melanie, still dazed from the impact, looked up in confusion. Her eyes widened in horror as realization dawned.

The metal stand she had collided with was no mere junk. It was a support, precariously holding up a stack of crushed cars that towered above them. And it was giving way.

Time seemed to slow as the mountain of twisted metal began to shift. Josh and Willie watched in frozen terror as the cars started to slide, picking up speed as they fell.

Melanie's scream was cut short as tons of rusted steel came crashing down. The sound was deafening – shrieking metal and shattering glass that seemed to go on forever.

Then, silence.

The grim reality of what had just occurred sank in. Where Melanie had stood moments before was now a mountain of crushed vehicles. There was no sign of movement, no cry for help. The finality of it was overwhelming.

Willie stumbled backwards, his face ashen. "I... I didn't mean to..." he mumbled, shock setting in.

Josh, his heart pounding, could only stare in disbelief. The narrow escape from death, and now this tragic turn of events – it was almost too much to process. Clint's ghost, who had been watching the scene unfold with eerie calm, finally spoke. His voice was softer now, tinged with a mix of satisfaction and what that might be regret.

"Ain't that something," he mused. "All these years, all her schemes... and in the end, it's the junkyard that got her. Poetic, if you ask me."

The wail of sirens grew louder. Red and blue lights began to illuminate the scene, casting surreal shadows across the piles of junked cars and the fresh site of tragedy.

Chapter 16

Free At Last

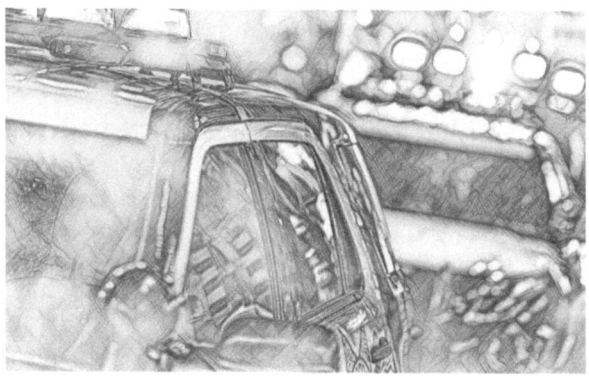

Red and blue lights sliced through the darkness, casting eerie shadows across the labyrinth of junked cars. The wail of sirens gave way to the crackle of police radios as a fleet of patrol cars surrounded Willie's Junkyard.

The scene buzzed with activity as officers cordoned off the area, their flashlights probing the shadows for any sign of disturbance.

Detective Sarah Ferguson stepped out of her unmarked sedan, her keen eyes taking in the controlled chaos around her. She'd seen her fair share of crime scenes, but something about this one made the hairs on the back of her neck stand up.

"What do we know so far?" she asked the nearest uniformed officer.

The young cop flipped open his notebook. "We got a 911 call about an hour ago. Caller said they heard screams coming from the junkyard. When we tried to make contact with the owner, no one answered. Given the history of the place..."

Ferguson nodded grimly. The junkyard had been on the department's radar for years, always skirting the edge of legality. "Any sign of the owner? Willie Barker?"

"Not yet, Detective. We're conducting a systematic search now."

As Ferguson was about to respond, a commotion at the police line caught her attention. Two young people – a man and a woman – were arguing heatedly with an officer, trying to push past the yellow tape.

"I don't care if it's an active crime scene!" the young man was saying, his voice tight with worry. "Our friend is in there somewhere!"

Ferguson made her way over, holding up her badge to the police officer. "I'm Detective Ferguson."

Daria spoke up, her eyes brimming with unshed tears. "It's us, Daria and Mike. We talked before. Our friend Josh came out here earlier today and we haven't heard from him since. He's not answering his phone, and his car is still here." She pointed to a classic Ford Mustang parked near the junkyard entrance.

Mike chimed in, his face a mask of concern. "Josh was looking into some weird stuff that was happening with his car. He thought the junkyard owner might have answers. Please, you have to let us help look for him!"

Ferguson studied the pair, sensing their genuine distress. After a moment's consideration, she made a decision. "Alright, you can come in, but you stay with me at all times. Understood?"

They nodded eagerly, ducking under the police tape.

As the expanded search party made their way into the junkyard, Ferguson couldn't shake the feeling that they were walking into something far more complex than a simple missing persons case. The air seemed charged with an unnatural tension, and whispers of an old ghost story associated with the junkyard tickled at the back of her mind.

"Josh!" Daria called out, her voice echoing off the piles of rusted metal. "Josh, where are you?"

Mike's flashlight beam danced across the junked cars, creating strange, shifting shadows. "Come on, buddy. Give us a sign here!"

As they pushed deeper into the maze of automotive relics, the sounds of the police activity at the entrance faded, replaced by an eerie silence. Ferguson felt as if they were being watched, though she couldn't spot anyone in the darkness.

Suddenly, a loud crash echoed through the junkyard, followed by a man's shout. All heads turned toward the sound.

"That came from the back, near the car compactor," Ferguson said, already breaking into a run. "Come on!"

As they raced toward the source of the commotion, none of them could have prepared for the scene they were about to encounter. The night's mysteries were about to unravel, and the truth – as strange and terrifying as it might be – would finally come to light.

As the search party's voices grew closer, Josh stumbled away from the horrific scene of Melanie's demise. His legs were weak, his mind reeling from the night's events. In his dazed state, he found himself drawn towards the spectral figure of Clint, who hovered at the edge of the junkyard's sodium lights.

"Hey, kid," Clint's ghostly voice was softer now, lacking the bitter edge it had held earlier. "You okay?"

Josh managed a weak nod, still struggling to process everything that had happened. "I... I think so. But Melanie, she's..."

Clint's translucent form shimmered, his expression a mix of satisfaction and something resembling peace. "Yeah, I know. Can't say I'm too broken up about it, all things considered."

For a moment, they stood in silence, the distant sounds of the search party growing louder. Then Clint spoke again, his voice taking on an otherworldly echo.

"Listen, Josh. I owe you one. You coming here, stirring things up... it did more than you know."

Josh looked at the ghost, confused. "What do you mean?"

Clint's form flickered, becoming momentarily more solid. "Melanie, she didn't just kill me. She bound me here, used some kind of dark mojo to keep my spirit tethered to this junkyard. All these years, I've been trapped, watching her schemes, unable to move on."

Understanding dawned on Josh's face. "And now?"

A smile spread across Clint's spectral features. "Now, thanks to you, that tether's been broken. Melanie's gone, and with her, whatever twisted power was holding me here."

As if to emphasize his point, Clint's form began to fade, the edges of his being becoming indistinct. Josh watched in amazement as the ghost grew more transparent with each passing second.

"You're... leaving?" Josh asked, a mix of relief and unexpected sadness in his voice.

Clint nodded, his form now barely visible. "It's time for me to go where I belong. Been waiting long enough."

Josh felt compelled to say something, to somehow acknowledge the bizarre bond they'd formed through this ordeal. "I hope you find peace, Clint."

The ghost's laughter, no longer menacing but filled with genuine mirth, echoed softly. "Peace? Nah, kid. Where I'm going, I'm hoping for a little rock 'n' roll."

With those final words, Clint's form dissipated completely, leaving behind nothing but a faint whisper on the wind and the lingering scent of leather and hair pomade.

Josh stood there, staring at the spot where Clint had been, a sense of awe washing over him. The night's horrors, the brush with death, the tangled web of past crimes and ghostly vengeance – it all seemed to crystalize in this moment of supernatural resolution.

The spell was broken by a shout from nearby. "Josh! Josh, are you there?"

Reality came crashing back as Josh recognized Mike's voice. The search party was close now. He turned towards the sound, ready to face whatever came next, knowing that explaining the night's events would be a challenge all its own.

As he moved to meet his rescuers, Josh cast one last glance over his shoulder at the empty space where Clint had vanished. The junkyard suddenly seemed quieter, as if a long-held breath had finally been released.

The beam of a flashlight cut through the darkness, landing squarely on Josh. He raised a hand to shield his eyes, his heart pounding as the footsteps grew closer.

"Josh! Oh my God, Josh!" Daria's voice broke with relief as she rushed forward, enveloping him in a tight embrace. Mike was right behind her, his face a mix of concern and confusion.

"What happened, man? Are you okay?" Mike asked, placing a steadying hand on Josh's shoulder.

Before Josh could formulate a response, the authoritative voice of Detective Ferguson cut through the night air. "Step back, please. Give him some space."

The detective approached, her keen eyes taking in Josh's disheveled appearance and the chaos of the scene behind him. In the distance, the sound of metal groaning and officers shouting orders created a cacophony of activity.

"I'm Detective Sarah Ferguson," she said, her tone professional but not unkind. "Are you injured, Josh? Do you need medical attention?"

Josh shook his head, still struggling to find his voice. "I'm... I'm okay. Just shaken up."

Ferguson nodded, then turned to address a nearby officer. "Johnson, secure the perimeter. I want every inch of this place searched. And get CSI down here ASAP."

As if on cue, two officers emerged from the maze of junked cars, leading a handcuffed Willie between them. The old man's head was bowed, his usual gruff demeanor replaced by a look of defeat.

"We found him trying to hide in an old bus, Detective," one of the officers reported.

Ferguson' eyes narrowed as she studied Willie. "Book him. We'll sort out the charges once we have a clearer picture of what went down here."

Turning back to Josh, the detective's expression softened slightly. "I know you've been through a lot tonight, but I'm going to need you to come down to the station to answer some questions. We need to understand exactly what happened here."

Josh turned back to Detective Ferguson. "What happened to Detective Reeves? I talked to him before."

Detective Ferguson paused for a moment, her stare growing more intense. "Retired," she responded sharply.

Mike stepped forward, protective instinct kicking in. "Can't this wait? He's clearly been through hell."

"I'm afraid not," Ferguson replied firmly. "Time is critical in cases like this. But don't worry, your friend isn't under arrest. We just need his statement while the events are still fresh."

Daria squeezed Josh's hand. "We'll come with you, Josh. You don't have to do this alone."

Josh nodded gratefully, the shock of the night's events still evident in his eyes. As Ferguson led them towards the police cars, the junkyard behind them bustled with activity. Officers combed the area, their flashlights illuminating the twisted metal and hidden corners of the property.

"Detective!" an officer called out. "You're going to want to see this. We've found... well, you should just come look."

Ferguson turned back, conflict clear on her face. "Alright," she said after a moment's hesitation. "Officer Clark, please escort Josh and his friends to the station. I'll be there shortly to take his statement."

As they were led away, Josh cast one last glance over his shoulder at the junkyard. In the harsh glare of police floodlights, the place looked different – no longer the realm of ghosts and dark secrets, but a crime scene being methodically picked apart.

The night's supernatural horrors were over, but Josh knew the ordeal was far from finished. As the police car pulled away, carrying him towards an uncertain future filled with questions and consequences, he couldn't help but wonder: how could he possibly explain what had really happened in Willie's Junkyard?

The boundary between the world of the living and the dead had been blurred tonight, and Josh found himself caught in the middle, tasked with bridging that impossible gap for those who would never understand.

Josh hoped that one day, long down the road, he'd be able to laugh about all that had happened. But not today. Today was the most emotionally exhausting time of his entire life.

Chapter 17

Revisiting Old Memories

The late autumn sun cast long shadows across Josh's bedroom as he sat on the edge of his bed, absently flipping through a stack of newspapers. His own face stared back at him from nearly every front page, alongside sensational headlines that seemed to grow more outlandish with each passing week.

"JUNKYARD HORROR: SMALL-
TOWN MECHANIC UNCOVERS
DECADES-OLD MURDER PLOT"

"GHOSTS, GRUDGES, AND GEARS:
THE TOPEKA TERROR THAT
SHOCKED THE NATION"

"SURVIVOR SPEAKS OUT: 'I SAW
DEATH IN THE SCRAPHEAP'"

Josh tossed the papers aside with a sigh. It had been six weeks since that fateful night in Willie's Junkyard, but the echoes of those events refused to fade. The media had latched onto the story with a fervor that surprised everyone, transforming the quiet Kansas town into the epicenter of a national obsession.

The official narrative, carefully crafted by the Topeka Police Department and eagerly disseminated by news outlets, painted a picture that was both simpler and more palatable than the truth. Josh had been labeled a victim, a young man who unwittingly stumbled upon a decades-old crime and narrowly escaped with his life. Willie, the gruff old junkyard owner, was cast as the primary suspect, his silence in the face of questioning only fueling speculation.

But Josh knew the truth was far more complex, far more unbelievable. The ghost of Clint, Melanie's betrayal, the supernatural forces at play – none of that had made it into the official reports. How could it? Even now, weeks later, Josh sometimes wondered if he had imagined it all.

A soft knock at the door pulled Josh from his reverie. "Come in," he called out, his voice still carrying a hint of the exhaustion that seemed to be his constant companion these days.

Mike poked his head in, concern etched on his features. "Hey, man. Just checking in. Daria's downstairs with some food if you're up for it."

Josh managed a weak smile. His friends had been his lifeline through all of this, a constant presence keeping him tethered to reality when the memories threatened to overwhelm him.

"Yeah, I'll be down in a minute. Thanks, Mike."

As his friend retreated, Josh's gaze fell on his dresser, where a small stack of business cards sat next to his keys. Therapists, counselors, support groups – all recommended by well-meaning doctors and police officers who assumed his trauma was solely from a brush with a murderous junkyard owner. How could he explain that his nightmares were filled not with Willie's gruff face, but with the ethereal glow of a vengeful spirit?

The media circus had brought with it a parade of self-proclaimed experts and paranormal investigators, all eager to cash in on the story. Josh had turned them all away, unable to stomach the thought of his experience being turned into fodder for reality TV or tabloid speculation.

Detective Ferguson had been a surprising source of support through it all. Though she clearly didn't believe the supernatural aspects of his story, she had kept those details out of the official reports, sparing Josh from even more intense scrutiny.

With a deep breath, Josh stood up, stretching muscles that felt perpetually tense. His '67 Mustang sat in the driveway, pristine and innocuous. He hadn't been able to bring himself to drive it since that night, the memory of Clint's spectral presence still too raw.

As he made his way downstairs to join his friends, Josh couldn't shake the feeling that the story wasn't over. The junkyard had been closed off, declared a crime scene, but he knew there were secrets still buried there, truths that might never see the light of day.

For now, though, he would focus on putting one foot in front of the other, on rebuilding some semblance of normalcy. The ghosts of the past – both literal and figurative – would have to wait. Josh had survived that night in the junkyard, and he was determined to do more than just survive its aftermath.

As the autumn days grew shorter, the investigation into the events at Willie's Junkyard continued behind closed doors. While the public narrative remained simplified, focusing on Willie as the primary suspect, a select few within the Topeka Police Department were privy to a far more complex and disturbing truth.

Detective Ferguson sat at her desk late one evening, poring over a confidential file. The overhead fluorescent lights cast a harsh glow on the photographs and reports spread before her. She rubbed her tired eyes, the weight of the unreleased findings heavy on her shoulders.

The truth, as they had pieced it together, was a tragedy of errors and desperate cover-ups. Melanie's mother had been the one to end Clint's life all those years ago. It hadn't been premeditated, but rather a horrific accident born of a heated argument.

According to recovered evidence and pieced-together testimonies, Melanie's mother and Clint had been fighting in his prized 1967 Ford Mustang – the same model Josh now owned. The argument had escalated, and in a moment of blind rage after they drove off, Melanie's mother grabbed the steering wheel and veered it into the tree. The evidence and pictured verified this after finding her hands stiffly gripped on the wheel.

Panicked and alone, Melanie had turned to the one person she thought she could trust: her grandfather Willie. Together, they had concocted a plan to hide the evidence. The junkyard, with its endless piles of twisted metal and forgotten vehicles, provided the perfect cover. They buried Clint there, deep among the automotive graves, and swore to take the secret to their own.

But secrets, like restless spirits, have a way of clawing their way to the surface.

Ferguson' eyes fell on a photograph of Josh's Mustang. By some twist of fate or cosmic joke, Josh had unknowingly purchased the very car in which Clint had met his end. The detective shuddered, recalling

Josh's insistence on the car being haunted. She pushed the thought aside, focusing instead on the facts she could prove.

The file contained detailed forensic reports, painstakingly reconstructed timelines, and statements from various witnesses who had known Clint, Melanie, and Willie back then. It painted a picture of young love turned toxic, of a tight-knit community where rumors simmered just below the surface, and of two people bound together by a terrible secret for decades.

What the file didn't contain – couldn't contain – was any official acknowledgment of the supernatural elements Josh had described. Ghosts, spiritual tethers, and spectral vengeance had no place in police reports or court documents. Those aspects of the story remained solely in Josh's testimony, carefully filed away separately from the main investigation.

Ferguson closed the file with a sigh. The truth they had uncovered was damning enough without venturing into the realm of the paranormal. Willie's role as an accessory after the fact, Melanie's years of deception, the web of lies that had finally unraveled – it was all more than enough for any jury to consider.

As for Josh's claims about Clint's ghost and the haunted Mustang, those would remain a matter of personal belief. Ferguson had seen enough in her career to keep an open mind, but she knew the department's official stance would always be one of skepticism towards anything supernatural.

The detective stood, stretching her stiff muscles. As she prepared to lock away the confidential file, she couldn't help but glance once more at the photo of Josh's Mustang. For a moment, she allowed herself to wonder: if objects could hold memories, what stories would that car tell? What echoes of the past might still linger in its steel and chrome?

Shaking off the unsettling thought, Ferguson secured the file and turned off her desk lamp. The full truth of what happened at Willie's Junkyard might never be known to the public. But for those involved, the repercussions would continue to ripple outward, touching lives in ways both seen and unseen, for years to come.

While the official investigation continued behind closed doors, Josh, Mike, and Daria had been conducting their own informal inquiry into the supernatural aspects of the case. On a crisp autumn evening, the three friends gathered in Mike's garage, surrounded by hastily scribbled notes, printouts of urban legends, and a corkboard covered in red string connecting various theories.

"So, let me get this straight," Mike said, pacing back and forth. "We think Clint's ghost was bound to the Mustang because that's where he died?"

Josh nodded, his eyes distant as he recalled the spectral encounters. "It makes sense. That car was Clint's pride and joy in life. If his death was tied to it..."

"Then it became his anchor in death," Daria finished, a shiver running down her spine despite the warmth of the garage.

They had spent weeks piecing together their theory, combining Josh's firsthand experiences with research into ghostly legends and paranormal phenomena. The conclusion they'd reached was both logical and chilling.

"But why did the hauntings only happen sometimes?" Mike asked, gesturing to a timeline they'd created. "Josh, you drove that car for months before anything weird started happening."

Josh leaned back in his chair, brow furrowed in thought. "I think... I think Clint only lashed out when someone was planning to do harm. Remember Darren?"

The other two nodded grimly. Darren had been a local troublemaker who had stolen Josh's Mustang a few months before the junkyard incident. He'd later been found by the side of the road, babbling about a ghostly figure in the backseat and swearing never to steal again.

"So Clint's ghost was what, some kind of supernatural vigilante?" Daria asked, her tone a mixture of disbelief and awe.

"More like a protector," Josh mused. "And with Melanie and Willie..." He trailed off, the memories still too fresh.

Mike placed a comforting hand on his friend's shoulder. "He was trying to bring their crimes to light. To find justice."

The three sat in silence for a moment, the weight of their conclusions settling over them. They knew their theory would sound absurd to anyone outside their circle, but for them, it was the only explanation that made sense of the inexplicable events they'd witnessed.

"So what now?" Daria finally asked, voicing the question they'd all been avoiding.

Josh stood up, walking over to the garage door. He pushed it open, revealing his Mustang sitting in the driveway. The classic car gleamed in the moonlight, beautiful and innocent-looking. But Josh knew better now.

"I can't keep it," he said softly. "Even if Clint's spirit has moved on, there's too much history there. Too many memories."

Mike and Daria exchanged glances, understanding the difficult decision their friend was making.

"You sure, man?" Mike asked. "That car meant a lot to you."

Josh nodded, his resolve firm. "It did. But after everything that's happened... I don't want to take any chances. Besides, maybe this way, Clint can finally rest in peace."

The next day, Josh contacted a classic car collector he'd met at a show the previous year. Within a week, the Mustang was sold, destined for a new home far from Topeka and the painful memories it held.

As Josh watched the car being driven away, he felt a mixture of sadness and relief. Part of him would always wonder if he'd made the right choice, if Clint's spirit had truly been laid to rest or if it would follow the Mustang to its new owner. But for now, at least, he could begin to move forward, leaving the ghosts of the past behind.

Mike and Daria stood beside him, offering silent support. They knew that while the official investigation might never acknowledge the supernatural elements of what had happened, the truth they had uncovered would stay with them always. It was a secret they would carry, a reminder of the thin veil between the world of the living and the realms beyond.

As the Mustang disappeared around a corner, Josh took a deep breath. The chapter of his life involving Clint,

Willie's Junkyard, and the haunted Mustang was finally closing.

Some time later, Josh found himself driving on the country road that led to Old Willie's Junkyard. He felt a need for closure, as if something was still unresolved in his mind. Josh veered in the direction of the junkyard, eventually arriving at the front. gate.

Albeit a struggle, Josh pushed the gates open, his heart already quickening. Twilight was settling over the sprawling maze of discarded metal and forgotten treasures. Josh swallowed hard, remembering why he'd sworn never to return.

But curiosity, that damnable curiosity, had brought him back.

The first few steps were the hardest. Gravel crunched beneath his feet, unnaturally loud in the eerie stillness. A cool breeze whispered through the skeletal frames of abandoned cars, carrying the acrid scent of oil and decay.

"Get it together," Josh muttered, clenching his fists. "There's nothing here."

Yet as he ventured deeper, that old, familiar chill began to creep up his spine. It was the same icy fingers he'd felt when Clint... No. Josh shook his head violently. Clint was gone. All of it was gone.

A sudden clang of metal on metal made him jump. Josh whirled, heart pounding, only to see a twisted piece of scrap settling into a new position. He laughed nervously, the sound brittle in the oppressive silence.

Shadows lengthened as Josh wandered, each step carrying him further into the labyrinth. The piles of junk loomed higher, their jagged silhouettes etched against the darkening sky. More than once, he thought he glimpsed movement from the corner of his eye, only to find nothing when he turned.

The wind picked up, moaning through the wrecks like a chorus of lost souls. Josh hugged himself, shivering despite the warm evening. Every instinct screamed at him to run, to flee this place of memories and lingering dread.

When a flock of startled crows erupted from a nearby heap with raucous cries, Josh finally broke. He sprinted for the entrance, heedless of the scratches from protruding metal and the sting of gravel kicked up by his pounding feet.

Only when the gates clanged shut behind him did Josh dare to look back. The junkyard stood silent and still, betraying nothing of the terror it held. Panting, he stumbled to his car, hands shaking as he fumbled with the keys.

"Never again," Josh swore, his voice hoarse. As he peeled away, tires squealing, he didn't see the lone figure watching from atop a mountain of crushed cars, its outline wavering in the gathering gloom.

In the distance, Josh felt another chill. He looked reluctantly one last time at the junkyard from his rear-view mirror. For a moment he thought he saw someone standing at the road entrance, but there was nothing when he relooked. Josh decided to focus his attention on the road ahead and try to gain a new sense of peace.

At the junkyard entrance, an apparition of Melanie formed, with the evilest smile on her face. She smiled wider, muttering to herself, "I'm coming for you, Josh."

THE END

CHECK OUT THESE OTHER NOVELS FROM NOBLE PARK

ABOUT THE AUTHOR

David Noble is a native of Tampa, Florida, By middle school he and a group of willing accomplices started making no-budget action movies, which would transition into a degree in Communications from the University of Tampa. In spite of joining the military, David found time to make several short films, turning to feature films by 2011. Over the years David has written, produced, and directed 'ZYDECO' (horror), 'Knight Squad' (martial arts), 'Secret Within The Sphere' (science fiction), and 'Lost Padre Mine' (adventure). These movies are available on many video streaming services today. David's visual works have been awarded and recognized in over 30 film festivals, some of which he has translated into novellas for your reading pleasure.

David Noble